THE LAST HAUNT

an oral history of the
MCKINLEY MANOR MASSACRE

MAX BOOTH III

CEMETERY GATES
MEDIA

The Last Haunt
Published by Cemetery Gates Media
Binghamton, New York

Copyright © 2023
By Max Booth III

All rights reserved. Without limiting the rights under the copyright reserved above, no part of this publication may be reproduced, stored in, or introduced into a retrieval system, or transmitted in any form or by any means (electronic, mechanical, photocopying, recording, or otherwise) without prior written permission.

ISBN: 9798861632836

For more information about this book and other Cemetery Gates publications, visit us at:

cemeterygatesmedia.com
twitter.com/cemeterygatesm
instagram.com/cemeterygatesm

Cover Art: Trevor Henderson

ALSO BY THE AUTHOR

Toxicity
The Mind is a Razorblade
How to Successfully Kidnap Strangers
The Nightly Disease
Carnivorous Lunar Activities
We Need to Do Something
Touch the Night
Maggots Screaming!
Abnormal Statistics

For my friend:

Jay Wilburn

(April 11, 1974 - October 18, 2022)

Chapter One

A Haunting in Texas

CHRISTINE ADDAMS, *neighbor of Gus McKinley*

I have no recollection of the day that cocksucker moved in.

This wasn't the kind of neighborhood where everybody knew everybody. Texas might have a reputation for its small towns sticking together, but that never felt true for Pork Basket. Sure, there was *some* sense of community, but there weren't nobody baking each other cookies on Christmas or getting together for barbecue cookouts in the summer. At least not on our street. If that kinda shit was happening elsewhere in town, we sure as hell weren't receiving any invitations. We kept to ourselves and life was just peachy.

Until that *sign* showed up in his front yard, anyhow. One day the front lawn was bare and then one day a sign was sticking out of it. Not a big sign, or anything too extravagant. It was a small, rectangular piece of cardboard with two steel poles stabbed into the dirt. The sort of sign you always see lawn care companies use.

MCKINLEY MANOR, it said. OPENING SOON.

Everything pretty much went to hell after that.

JOHN BALTISBERGER, *retired cop*

The first time we got a call about Gus, I about shit my pants. I don't feel any shame in admitting that now, all these years later. It's the truth. The way Barb sounded on the radio, you'd think her own family had just gotten hacksawed up into a bunch of little pieces. "Get down there, Johnny!" she screamed into the radio, so loud I'm still surprised I ain't get deaf from it. "They're killin' 'em! They're killing *all* of 'em!"

Naturally, I had some questions. Such as *who* was killing *who*, exactly? But of course she didn't know that. And why would she, right? It wasn't her job to know. It was mine to find out. It came with the job description, and all.

Now, Pork Basket, it ain't exactly a town flooding with crime activity. Nothin' much ever happens here. Or, at least that *was* the case before Gus moved in and started all his Halloween nonsense. Back then it was a nice, safe town any good Christian would be proud to call home. Nobody got murdered. At least not in the horror movie way. Sometimes husbands got drunk and beat their wives to death but that wasn't abnormal, that was just life.

Gus, on the other hand, now that was what I'd describe as abnormal. Heck, you look up the word in the dictionary, and they wouldn't have a definition printed. Merely his face, and that creepy dead-eyed smile of his. Around these parts, you didn't get more abnormal than Gus McKinley. But I reckon that was why he ended up being so successful. Well, before all the bad stuff happened to him, at least. But even then, I betcher he'd have some backwaters way of looking at the bad stuff…uh…optimistically. Most snake oil salesmen do, don't they? [*Laughs.*]

It was about mid-afternoon, I reckon, so the traffic wasn't nothing to worry about. I didn't even have to put on my siren, tell you the truth. Got there in no time at all. The street—well, everybody knows the street now—but back then it was still considered tame. It looked normal. The kinda place any good law-abiding American would want to live. Gus's house, though, I do admit it had its peculiarities. Although back in those early days it looked more like a child's birthday party than what it would eventually become.

That's how it looked when I got there that day. A child's birthday party, I mean. There was a sign staked out in the front lawn that said MCKINLEY MANOR, and he had little lines of ribbon hung up from nearby trees connecting to the front of the house. It wasn't until later that I realized each ribbon was painted to look bloodstained. Aside from a few plastic skeletons and pumpkin props, a zombie gnome here and there, that was about as *spooky* as the outside got.

I grabbed my radio, about to check in with Barb and confirm this was the right address—would hate to bother someone with something like this and it ain't even the place I was meant to go—when sure enough, I heard the same thing the neighbors had been hearing all morning.

A woman screaming.

Not just any scream, either. This was one of the worst screams I'd ever heard in my life, and that's saying a lot, don't you think? Considering my profession and all. But this scream…my god, it was the scream of someone convinced they was about to die. A scream of complete and total *terror*.

Followed by the sound of a chainsaw.

CHRISTINE ADDAMS

Come on. Of course I was the one who called the cops on his ass. It wouldn't be the last time, either. And it wasn't like I was shy about it. I proudly told him I was the one who'd done it. All our other neighbors were way too chickenshit to pick up the phone. You think they'd confront the fuckhead directly? Fat chance. Not me, though. Over time, I made it my business to piss this miserable bastard off.

JOHN BALTISBERGER

Well, what do you think I did when I got to Gus's house? I'm a police officer. I swore an oath. You think I'm one of those crooked cops or something? One of those *corrupt pigs* conceived by Black Lives Matter thugs? No sir. You give me a job and I do my job. That's all there is to it. Simple as that.

I got out of my car and, once I was sure I hadn't made a mess in my trousers, I headed toward the source of the scream—which was behind the house, in the back yard. I didn't bother knocking on the front and announcing my presence. Whatever was going on here, I knew it was nothin' good, and me showing up would only, uhh...*exacerbate* the situation. It'd be better to catch 'em by surprise, was my train of thought. After all, it's not like I wasn't rich with probable cause at that point, right?

So I snuck through the unlocked gate and I made my way around the house. The whole time the woman kept on screaming over the chainsaw. A real piercing scream that gave me an instant headache. By then I could make out actual words coming from her wails. Stuff like *help me* and *please* and *let me go*. Real horror movie stuff, you know?

Now, the back yard wasn't as innocent looking as the front had been, although it was still a long ways from evolving into its final form. The props were at least more realistic back here. Decapitated heads that didn't look like they were bought at Walmart. Blood stains that weren't too bright like movie blood, but *real* blood. I shrugged most of it off as Halloween decorations, since we were already a couple weeks into October by then, but what I *couldn't* shrug off were the noises coming from the shed on the other side of the yard.

I stood outside the shed for a good twenty seconds with my gun drawn before I made the decision to open it. Pains me to admit it now, but there was absolutely a big part of me that was too chickenshit to go through with it. I kept trying to convince myself to hang back, to radio in backup, wait for some more bodies. But that ain't what happened. Despite what the situation ended up being, *at the time* I had no way of knowing that. *At the time* I sincerely thought there was a real goddamn maniac in there. And I still opened the door, all by my lonesome, and for that, I am proud of myself. Not everybody has the balls to do something like that. Most cops don't, I'll tell you that. But I did.

And what did I find in this shed? Well, about what I expected. I found a woman, chains wrapped around her wrists, hanging her from the ceiling. I found a man with a pillowcase over his head, eye holes crudely cut in the middle of the fabric. He was standing behind her, holding a mini chainsaw in one hand and a melting popsicle in the other. And what else did I find? I found a slab of beef burning on a hotplate, is what I found.

Whatever any of that could mean, my brain refused to register. So I aimed the pistol at the guy—who of course turned out to be Gus—and told him to drop his weapons and get on the ground. To his credit, he obliged. He dropped the popsicle, then turned off the chainsaw and lowered it to his feet. The woman was still screaming, but the tone of her wailing had changed. It sounded more hopeful now. Grateful I'd come to put an end to whatever bizarre crap was going on down here.

"Please," she screamed at me, "please help, he's going to kill me!"

"It's okay," I told her. "Everything's okay."

And, as it turned out, I wasn't bullshitting her like I usually do. Everything *was* okay.

Yes, Gus had a real chainsaw, but not once had it ever made contact with the woman's flesh. She was chained up and unable to look behind her, so realistically she had no idea what was going on. She had to rely on her other senses to tell the story, which Gus was taking full advantage of. The chainsaw was a prop, like everything else. Every time he revved it, what he did was take the popsicle and press it against the woman's bare back—he'd ripped a hole in her shirt for this very reason—so the sudden *coldness* of the popsicle would trick her brain into interpreting the sensation as extreme heat rather than…the opposite. That, on top of the smell of beef burning on the hotplate, convinced her that she was really being sawed into. It's brilliant, if you think about it, in a sick sort of way. Which is the only way one *can* appreciate what Gus does—or, I guess, *did.*

Later, I'd ask him where he got an idea like that, and he said he saw it in a movie once. Which is where it'd turn out he got most of his ideas.

Movies.

HOWIE MCKINLEY, *father of Gus McKinley*

Oh yeah, Gus had been into all that horror movie nonsense since he was a kid. Don't ask me who introduced him to it, because I ain't got the faintest. Other kids at school, if I was forced to wager. Sometimes he'd come home with those gory monster magazines and show me the most disgusting pictures you've ever seen and say stuff like, "Isn't this the coolest?" And I'd always tell him the same thing: "Goddammit, Gus, I'm trying to eat dinner here!"

You see, he thought it was real funny to try grossing me out while we was eating. Everything was always a game to him somehow. Dinner especially. He couldn't eat and watch TV with me like a normal kid. Instead he had to come up with these little challenges. Could he make me lose my appetite? Could he play around with his food until it looked grotesque?

Gus was born in '73, just in time for when all those godawful slashers theaters started shitting out like diarrhea a decade later. At first I tried resisting and telling him no, that he couldn't go see 'em—but when Gus was determined about something, let me tell you, he found a way to make it happen. I don't remember what his favorites were, so don't ask. Look, to me, all that shit was the same thing over and over. Guys with masks chopping up naked bimbos or what have you. I didn't understand the appeal. I still don't. But Gus? Gus couldn't get enough of it. Every new picture, he *had* to see. And not only one, no sir. He'd go back multiple times and watch the same pictures over and over. That was the kind of kid Gus was.

Now, if you want to know whether or not he was going to the movies alone or with friends, I'm afraid I gotta tell you something about my son. My son didn't *have* friends. Sure, sometimes he hung out with other kids. But they weren't his *friends*. To be quite frank with you, sir, I doubt Gus ever had a real friend in his life. It wasn't something he seemed all that interested in. Achieving a personal connection with someone like that.

Yeah, him and Debbie were married for a while there, but as I'm sure you already know, it wasn't like the marriage *lasted* or anything. Would he have ever considered his wife a friend? I think he would have laughed if you'd posed the question. I think he would have said something like, *What the hell is that supposed to mean?*

Debbie, though? How would she answer such a question? Now, *that* I do wonder.

DEBORAH KEATON, *ex-wife of Gus McKinley*

I met Gus shortly after he got out of the Navy. We got married less than a year later, after we found out I was pregnant with Charlie. It wasn't exactly a shotgun marriage, or anything, but at the same time it wasn't *not* that either. Would I have married him otherwise? [*Long pause.*]

To describe him as a weirdo would have been an understatement. Gus is the most unusual man I've ever known in my life. I was only nineteen when we first got together. Gus was how old? There was something bizarre and mysterious about him that I'd never seen in another man my age. His whole demeanor was off-kilter. He had no interest in sports, which I found refreshing. All he ever wanted to do was go to the movies or rent video tapes.

Don't get me wrong. I loved movies too. But he never wanted to do anything else except screw around every now and then—and that was only after *I* had to initiate something. Make the first move. I found that refreshing too, at first. The fact that he wasn't always trying to climb all over me any time we hung out. But after a while you start to wonder if something's wrong with you, you know what I mean? You start wondering what does he love more—you, or these goddamn horror movies? Because that was all he ever wanted to watch.

Now, don't go thinking I'm a prude. I never *disliked* horror or anything. In fact I'd say that was what drew me and him together in the first place, this shared love of the genre. But Gus was obsessed with it. Anything else he viewed as a waste of time.

Actually, thinking about it, I guess horror *is* how we met—uh, in a way. It won't seem so controversial now, but back then it sure raised quite the fuss. Before we ever met up face to face, Gus and I first started talking online. Are you old enough to remember AOL? The chatrooms back then! [*Laughs.*] Gosh, they could get really crazy, you know, like really chaotic. I don't spend so much time online now except for Facebook. All this internet stuff has gotten a little too complicated for me. Or maybe my brain is dying like brains tend to do. But back in the '90s, chatrooms were simple and relatively easy to figure out. Any monkey with a keyboard could participate. Including Gus.

I don't remember exactly what the conversation was about that drew the two of us together. Definitely something horror movie related. It would have been a chatroom dedicated to that stuff. Those were the ones I tended to haunt the most.

[*Shivers.*]

Sorry. I can't stand that word anymore. *Haunt.* Another thing Gus ended up ruining—my own vocabulary. Not to mention any love I may have once held for horror movies.

You want to hear something sad? Like, really truly depressing?

I don't even like Halloween anymore.

I can't do it. The whole season makes me sick to my stomach. I wasn't always like that, I can assure you. Like many others, Gus changed me for the worst.

HOWIE MCKINLEY

I wasn't surprised at all when I found out he was opening up his own haunted house. It wasn't like this was the first one he'd ever tried. Back when he was a boy, he would spend every night and weekend in our garage, fooling around with building his own spooky decorations. He'd create these elaborate little haunts and put up a sign in our front yard every Halloween. Nobody ever came. But he didn't give up, no sir, he kept at it every year. And I know for a fact this continued after he joined the Marines. He told me all about it in the letters he'd mail back home, how when everybody was bored he'd devise ways to scare the other men, and they loved it. Now, he *said* they loved it. Did they really? I don't know about that. I once heard him tell people *I* loved it when he'd gross me out during dinnertime, and that certainly couldn't have been further from the truth. But that was Gus for you, and I loved him.

MIGUEL MYERS, *veteran haunter*

I've designed and hosted my own haunts for the past thirty, thirty-five years all throughout the country. Long before Gus McKinley came on the scene, and long after he left. When someone gets involved in haunts, it becomes more than just a hobby. It becomes a lifestyle. My closest friends in the world are fellow haunters. Heck, it's how I met my wife. We go to the conventions together, we post on the same message boards—I think you get the picture. And in my time as a haunter, I've come to learn that every haunted house is different. Many of them share similar qualities, but they all have their own personalities. They value different things. Boo haunts, for example, focus their target audience on families. They embrace child-friendly scares. These haunted houses aren't designed to actually spook anybody. Instead, they are more focused on everybody having a fun time.

DEBORAH KEATON

I thought the haunted house idea was cute at first. That was back when it was for little kids, though. A boo haunt, isn't that what it's called? I helped him put it together and everything. It was something we bonded over. Making the decorations and figuring out what would be scary but not *too scary*. I remember we spent a lot of time in that kitchen in those early days, coming up with the perfect dishes that might feel the most like eyeballs and guts and other disgusting bodily organs. We'd blindfold the kids and have them stick their fingers in the bowls and tell them they were touching intestines. Sometimes the kids would go, "Ooh, that's so gross!" and sometimes they'd laugh with glee. It was all very…*innocent*. If things had stayed like that, who knows, we might've stayed married.

BETTY ROCKSTEADY, *moderator of the MCKINLEY MANOR OFFICIAL!!! Facebook community group*

I guess, so we're not wasting each other's time, it's best if I get something out of the way right up front. I was deeply, irrevocably in love with Gus McKinley. I had been for many years. Although I admit I hadn't always felt that way about him. This wasn't exactly a love at first sight kind of thing. I like to sometimes joke that it was *fright* at first sight. [*Laughs.*] I know not everybody likes puns, but I do, and you know who else did? Gus. Another thing we had in common—another thing of many.

The first day I ever met Gus McKinley, he tied me up in his shed and pretended to torture me with a chainsaw. I screamed so loud, some noisy neighbor ended up calling the cops on us and they came and broke it all up.

Before that day, we'd only spoken a few times on Facebook. He had reached out to me first, actually. Although…to be fair, I did instigate things a little. This was back when he was still doing the boo haunts. Are you familiar with boo haunts? Basically, as Gus used to say, "kid shit." Flannels and blue jeans stuffed with hay. Pumpkins with scary face paint. The kind of thing you can take a baby to, you know what I mean?

Of course, I never actually *attended* one of them. But I saw pictures and videos posted on the McKinley Manor Facebook page. The *old* McKinley Manor Facebook page. Before it got a necessary reboot, thanks to yours truly. Back then, hardly anyone at all interacted with his posts. Felt like he was screaming into the void, begging for anyone to pay attention to him, to acknowledge all the hard work he'd put into this haunt. And maybe a part of me intuited that desperation. Some small-peckered cupid angel drowned somewhere in my subconsciousness.

So I started commenting. I started *antagonizing*. Saying shit like not even babies could get spooked from this Disney-rated garbage. Since I was the only one replying outside of a few bourgeois soccer moms, it didn't take but an hour or so before I fell on his radar. We found ourselves in a little bit of a flame war after that. Which was exciting. Exciting and a little hot. It's fun to argue with strangers on the internet. Don't let anybody ever tell you differently.

Before long, he slid up into my DMs. Real confrontational and masculine. I was instantly attracted to the vibe, despite being in denial about it. Back then, I wasn't the most open or adventurous when it came to exploring my sexuality. That changed the more I got to know Gus, of course, but this was still in our early beginnings, and I misunderstood the warmth in my stomach for something else. I thought we were *feuding*. I didn't realize we were actually *flirting*. Although, with Gus, sometimes those two words were entirely antonymous.

DEBORAH KEATON

Gus was always sensitive to criticism. Trust me, I was the one who had to live with him. I heard it all. When that Facebook girl started giving him a hard time about the boo haunts, it was all he could talk about. You would have thought he was being prosecuted by the state, the way he was acting. So defensive and paranoid.

Of course, over the years of our marriage, I learned "defensive and paranoid" was Gus's natural state of being. Anything else was well-worn camouflage.

He decided to start taking things more…extreme. He spent a lot of time online, "researching" as he called it, trying to figure out a way to revitalize the Manor. Naturally, he read about other extreme haunts. The kind of haunts that made headlines. Places that allow the actors to touch the guests, to really invade their personal space.

That's when he invited the Facebook girl over and did the thing with the chainsaw and got the cops called.

By the way, I wasn't home when this happened. He told me nothing about his plans. I had to hear about it later, from a friend of a friend who heard about what happened from their second cousin. You know how these things tend to spread. It's embarrassing.

BETTY ROCKSTEADY

I've never forgotten the first DM he ever sent me. I think about it a lot, especially when I'm in bed and can't sleep and I'm feeling lonesome.

"You wanna get scared, little girl?"

He called me *little girl*. I remember seeing that message for the first time and feeling an instant wetness. Suddenly all the sarcasm I'd been using in the comments on his posts vanished. "Yes," I typed back, and awaited further instructions. I didn't dare take my eyes away from my phone until he followed up an hour later. He told me he had taken my and some others' feedback to heart, and he'd decided to rebuild his haunt from the ground up. Gone was all the kid shit, he said. That's not what people wanted. People wanted to get scared. They wanted things to get extreme. Well, he could do that, but first he needed some volunteers to help him work out the kinks.

Which was why he was messaging me. He wanted me to come down to his house, to the Manor, to go through a test run with him. He had some ideas, he told me, that were a little controversial, but he was positive they would completely change the game.

He told me that he was going to be, and I quote, "the Michael Jordan of haunts."

At the time, maybe it sounded a little silly, sure, but c'mon, let's be honest here. Was he *wrong*? Or is that not exactly what he ended up becoming? When you think of haunts, who is the first name to come to mind? Can you even *think* of a second person?

Because I sure can't.

DEBORAH KEATON

After the chainsaw incident, he started getting serious about recruiting actors. If his haunt was step it up, he couldn't handle everything himself, which was how he'd been managing the boo haunts.

You have to understand, he began doing this whole thing as a fun hobby on Halloween for the neighborhood kids. He never pretended like it was this serious thing, until suddenly it *was*, until it was the most serious thing he'd ever been a part of, and then he was saying things like it had to be the best haunt in the world and acting like people were counting on him not to fail them. Why did it have to be, though? And who were these *people*? I never asked him that, not directly. I doubt he would have had an answer that made sense, anyway. Once Gus got something in his head, there was no unraveling it. It was just the way it was.

The actors were mostly teenagers. I don't know how he found them. They weren't theater kids, or anything like that. More like burnouts. Stoners and petty thieves. Anyone he could get to work for free, because we certainly couldn't afford to hire anyone. As I'm sure you know, Gus never made any money from these haunts. From the very beginning, he always charged the same thing.

The funny thing is, we never even had any dogs.

MIGUEL MYERS

It's not controversial to claim one of the biggest factors contributing to Gus McKinley's popularity was his refusal to accept monetary compensation. Pretty much every haunt, especially *extreme* haunts, charge cash. But not McKinley.

Instead, he required one fifty-pound bag of dog food per guest.

The Last Haunt

Which, I would wager, is universally agreed upon as unusual—at least when you first hear about it. You have this retired Marine in Texas hosting one of the most extreme haunts in the country, with a waitlist in the thousands, and all he's charging is a bag of dog food? People might start questioning his motives. Is he sincerely doing all of this for the love of the haunt? If so, that would make him no different than most haunters. This is absolutely a business you must love to death or else it's going to crush you and break you until you're nothing.

But still. Why dog food, one might wonder? Does he have a lot of dogs, perhaps? No, of course not. McKinley never had a dog in his life. He was allergic.

All of the dog food was reportedly donated to local animal shelters.

Now, I've been involved in the haunt scene for most of my life, and at conventions us haunters tend to gossip. For a while there, McKinley was talk of the town, especially because he never attended any of the cons or socialized with other haunters. He viewed us all as competition, as the *enemy*. Very silly, I know, but silly men believe silly things.

But that was okay, because his absence provided us ample freedom to—pardon my language—talk shit. None of us cared for him, yet there was a certain charm to his mystique that we found irresistible. Quite frankly, he was impossible not to analyze. Which is why, I imagine, we're still talking about him now, and why you have decided to compile this oral history in the first place.

The dog food gimmick, that always got brought up, usually with the most cynical speculation conceivable.

Because he avoided participating in any monetary transactions, he was never legally required to operate as a business. And, when you aren't *legally* a business, you are able to skirt around certain regulations. You aren't obligated to practice the same health and safety standards more legitimate haunts might be bound to. Which, for example, is how he got away without having an established safe word for so long.

Moreover, accepting dog food in lieu of cash and then donating the dog food to animal shelters gave him the pretense of being a charity, which was a whole other safety blanket he could hide under should any controversy or criticism befall the Manor.

Or maybe the man simply loved dogs.

Who's to say?

ZACH CHAPMAN, *haunt actor*

I was one of the first actors Gus took on. He saw something in me. I know that because that's what he told me. All those years ago, after we first started getting to know each other, he put a hand on my shoulder and he said, "Son, I see something in you." Ain't ever forgot that. My piece-of-shit old man sure as hell never said nothing like that to me. Gus was a better dad than the shitbird who spurted me out of his dirty dick, that's for damn sure.

How we met…you know, it's a funny story.

I was sixteen. In and out of school. Suspended for one bullshit reason after another bullshit reason. You know how teachers can get. Once they decide they ain't like you there's no use botherin' with 'em anymore. You so much as open your mouth or look at 'em funny and suddenly they got fifteen different reasons to write you up. So, naturally, like anybody in my position, I decided fuck school. To hell with 'em. What good's school ever been for someone like me, anyhow? Right? Right? So I stopped going. I stopped giving a shit. And you know what? So did they. Not once did anyone call home and inquire about my absence. If anything, they must've been relieved when I didn't return after my last suspension ended. And it wasn't like my old man could give a shit, either. If it

The Last Haunt

wasn't a can of Lone Star then it didn't concern him. To hell with him, too. Maybe he was a better man back when Mom was still alive, but I never got to meet that man, so what's the use in yearnin' for shit you ain't even know about? You know what I mean?

So what was I doing if I wasn't going to school, you might be wondering? What any sixteen-year-old dropout would be up to, if given the opportunity. Fucking anybody who'd move. Stealing anything not nailed down. Crashing on any couch that wouldn't give me lice. Some of the best years of my life, all right. I say that as an absolute fact. Nowadays, shit's all different. I'm on parole for how fuckin' many more years? Plus I got a kid of my own now, and he's a real fuckin' asshole, let me tell you. But at least I pay attention to him. At least I *try*. Can't say that about my dad. Nobody could say that about him.

But back then, I was living the dream. Not a goddamn care in the world, I tell you. There was a Walmart open twenty-four-seven back then. I haven't seen anything open all night like that since before China tried to sabotage us all with the plandemic, come to think about it. What the hell are all these businesses waiting for? Ain't they heard Covid's long over? Anyway. There's this Walmart on the edge of town, and back when I was sixteen I'd break into cars in the parking lot. Nobody was patrolling shit and ninety-nine percent of the cameras didn't work. If you were smart and struck at the right moment, ain't nobody could do shit about it. I stole so much back then. Some of it I kept. Most of it I hocked. Dude at the pawnshop and I were on a first-name basis, if you know what I mean.

Only time I ever got caught, though? Guess who.
Our boy Gus.

I still don't know where the hell he came from. Must have been one, two in the morning. Only a few cars here and there. Nobody in sight, practically a ghost town. There's this

19

pickup I set my sights on. Gus's pickup, it turns out. A decent one, too. I got my gear with me. I don't need to break windows, but I will if I have to. Luckily, in this instance, I was able to jimmy the lock no sweat. And it's when I'm ass-up, digging through the glovebox, that I hear someone clear their throat behind me, and I know I'm fucked.

"Howdy," he says, all amused and sure of himself. First thing I ever hear him say, before I can even lay eyes on him. Fuckin' *howdy*. Ain't that a hoot?

But he didn't turn me in. Didn't so much as threaten to get the cops involved. That kind of stuff—the law—it never seemed to faze him one way or the other.

Instead, he asked if I wanted to get some coffee with him. Who was I to say no, right? He busted me redhanded and outweighed me by at least a hundred-and-fifty pounds— most of it muscle, too. Don't forget, Gus used to be a Marine. Those crazy sons of bitches are built differently.

So, yeah. We got in his truck and he drove to a nearby Denny's. Dude bought me one of those...what do you call them? Fuckin'...moons over my hammy? Goddamn, I ain't had one of those in a minute. Anyway. I don't need to get into everything we talked about there, but I'll tell you this. By the end of the night, he offered me the opportunity of a lifetime.

CHRISTINE ADDAMS

Shortly after the first incident that led to me calling the cops on his ass, I started seeing more and more people hanging out at his house. Teenage boys, mostly. My initial instinct was to assume he had some sort of deviant sex ring going on, and I want to be clear that I haven't entirely ruled that theory from suspicion, but I soon surmised that these boys were Gus's hired help. I often spotted them setting up displays, hanging signs, wearing those ridiculous pillowcases on their heads.

Every one of them avoided me like the plague, too, which I found funny. Clearly Gus had instructed them not to associate with me. Lord knows the rumors that creep spread about the "crazy lady across the street."

BETTY ROCKSTEADY

I would have killed to be an actor. Seriously. I would have murdered any hobo in the state of Texas for a chance to act in Gus's Manor. And it wasn't like he didn't want me involved, either. I was one of the first people he offered a role. Unfortunately, the timing wasn't perfect. College was beginning soon. I was leaving town. It wouldn't work out. An insane part of me considered blowing off school altogether so I could stay and help the Manor grow, but I think my parents would have skinned me alive. In the end, I definitely made the right decision, because my physical absence led to Gus giving me a way more important job—in my opinion, the most essential job there was when it came to the Manor. He made me moderator of the Facebook group.

DEBORAH KEATON

Just hearing the word "Facebook" these days is enough to raise my blood pressure. Sometimes all it takes is seeing the color blue to make me see red. In the final years of our marriage, I saw more of him through his Facebook statuses than I did face-to-face. If he wasn't outside doing something haunt-related, he was secluded in his office hunched over the computer. Meanwhile I was stuck raising our son practically by myself, not to mention taking care of trivial housework, doing all the cooking, and also working a full-time job. Which is funny, or downright depressing, when you remember at this point Gus was technically retired. He wouldn't start working at Walmart until after the divorce was finalized and he could no longer mooch off my paychecks. Another reason why, once I was no longer in the picture, you'll notice the decline in production value on his haunts. He couldn't afford the upkeep on set design. When we were married, I was the one paying for everything.

BETTY ROCKSTEADY

Gus and I talked a lot via DM and on video calls about how to construct the group. He was the one who suggested it should be private. The idea being that the mystery aspect of the whole thing is what would really pique people's interest. In those early days, the group was bare bones. Only a couple Pork Basket locals had joined after Gus posted invite links on his personal profile and also the soon-to-be-extinct page he'd made for the lame boo haunts. But Gus was a genius, you know? He knew to gain any real traction, he'd have to start recording the new-and-improved haunts. And he was right. It wasn't until a few of the videos went viral on YouTube that the Facebook group started exploding with requests to join. He'd included links to the group on all the videos. Shit was working exactly as he predicted it would.

SUSAN SNYDER, *former haunt participant*

I don't know what happened. Suddenly I couldn't stop vomiting. They had me in the barrel where they were doing the waterboarding, and something triggered my gag reflex, I guess, and I started spewing everywhere. All over the barrel. Through my mouth. Through my nose. It burned so bad, I remember thinking, before the smell hit, zeroing in on how much it *hurt* to puke like that. I was blindfolded but I knew everybody was pleased with what they'd caused. They were all laughing. *Giggling*. One of them said, in this psychotic sing-song voice, "*What goes out must go back in*," and before I could comprehend what that might've meant, they were dunking my face into the barrel. They said if I didn't open my mouth and slurp up my mess, they would kill me. They said they'd drown me in my own puke and everybody watching at home would turn me into a laughingstock. They said I'd become a meme. They said they had killed people at this Manor before and they had no problem doing it again—especially when it came to stupid girls like me, who couldn't control their bodily functions. And, in that moment, I believed them. I completely, one-hundred percent believed them. And, you know what? I still do.

JOHN BALTISBERGER

Gus and I were forced to work out a system, to come to an understanding of some kind. I mean, we had to, ya know? Otherwise there would've never been any goddamn peace. I knew what he was doing. I didn't *understand it*, but I knew enough that he wasn't technically breaking any laws, and the folks he was torturing and whatnot, they'd signed up for it, they'd agreed to…you know, the torturing…and, uh, whatnot. So what we agreed to was, any time he was planning another one of his little Halloween shenanigans, he'd warn the station ahead of time. That way, if anybody around the area complained about someone screaming or being killed or what have you, we knew it would be okay to simply dismiss it as another theatric. Our police force was operating under limited resources. We couldn't afford the gasoline every time someone got a little spooked.

CHRISTINE ADDAMS

The Manor was a plague on our neighborhood. The moment he stuck the sign out in his front yard, I knew it was bad news. I'm no prude, but I have my limits. Gus McKinley was a sick fuck, and this Manor of his was an excuse to get off on his perverted torture fantasies. He'd asked me a few times if I would consider doing it. He said I could skip the waitlist and everything, since we were neighbors. I told him if he so much as rung my doorbell again, I would not hesitate in shooting his ass for trespassing. This being Texas and all, I would've been well within my rights, too.

ZACH CHAPMAN

There were four of us to start with. All male. All around the same age. All with…similar disregard of the law. We were punks. Petty fuckin' crooks. Real goddamn losers. It was a glorious time to be alive.

I was the first one Gus recruited, but the other three soon followed. There was me, then there was Rick, then Frank, then Trey. People liked to call us the McKinley Boys, like we were a fuckin' gang or something, but truthfully none of us got along all that well. Trey especially was a little asshole. And Frank? One of the biggest pussies I ever met. If not for Gus we would have never crossed paths. I'm not surprised he refused to speak to you, either. He likes to pretend like he was never involved in the Manor. Afraid of getting cancelled or whatever the fuck. Cowardly behavior, if you ask me.

I don't know, exactly, how Gus found the others. I imagine the same way I entered his life. He caught them doing something they should've have, and instead of fetching the cops he asked them to come help with the Manor. My wife tries telling me what he did was technically blackmail, but she don't get it. She wasn't there. She didn't know him. Her and I didn't become acquainted until after I was paroled. Sure, okay, maybe it *sounds* like blackmail, from an outsider's perspective. But that wasn't the type of guy Gus was. We could have said no. We could have told him to eat shit. I don't think he would have gotten the authorities involved if we'd declined his offer. There was never any…*threat.* It was more like an opportunity. Like, hey man, I know you're having a rough go at it, why don't you consider changing things up at my haunted house? That kind of thing.

And you know what? We were grateful.

BETTY ROCKSTEADY

I made it a point to watch as many livestreams as my schedule allowed, but it never felt like the real thing. The boys who worked for him, I consider them the true lucky ones. You know what I would have given for the opportunity to waterboard some weak piece of shit at Gus's command?

Usually, after a haunt Gus would give me a call to sort of regroup on how the night had gone, since he could count on me to monitor the stream. I'd give him tips on how to make stuff more extreme, let him know what I thought wasn't working, and he'd tell me about all of his worries, his aspirations, his dreams.

The phone calls increased in length once his wife ran out on him. That really devastated him, believe it or not. He sincerely loved that ugly bitch. Thankfully I was there—in a matter of speaking—to comfort him. I never in a million years expected our phone calls to take the route they took. I'd *hoped* for it, sure, but I never truly believed Gus would want me in the same way I wanted him.

It got to a point where minutes after a stream ended, Gus

would be rushing inside his house and dialing my number, out of breath, pants already around his ankles. And I'd be waiting for him, hand between my legs. Waiting for him to tell me what he was going to do to me. All the fucked-up horror shit he could imagine. I welcomed it, even if I begged him to let me go, even if I told him I was going to call the police. He told me there was no escape. He told me he was going to kill me. He told me he was going to erase my very existence.

I've never gotten off like I did during those late-night phone calls. Not before, and not since. Nobody on this earth can make me wet like Gus did. Sometimes it's those orgasms I miss most of all.

And, since I'm in the sharing mood, I'll go ahead and disclose that I do in fact still have many of those old streams saved on a hard drive, and they've one-hundred percent cured me from certain extreme bouts of loneliness on long, sleep-deprived nights. Just last week I fell asleep masturbating to the audio of Gus promising to murder someone's family.

That's the beauty of those videos, you know? Gus might be dead, sure, but he still *lives on*. He survives through his legacy.

And that, to me, is hot as fuck.

ZACH CHAPMAN

He used to invite us over for lunch every so often. All four of us. Nothing, like, extravagant. It would've been cool if he'd dished out on some pizzas, but Gus was never someone with a lot of money, and neither were we, but that was okay. We were content to have sandwiches and chips. He'd also give us beer, which we thought was cool.

I know what you might be thinking. I've heard the rumors, okay? What were four teenaged boys doing over at this grown man's house all the time? Giving them beer and

The Last Haunt

being all secretive. Was he some kind of *fruitcake?* Was he diddlin' them all? Was McKinley Manor some kind of...de*praved* sex cult? Come the fuck on. You really buy into that stupid bullshit? What about his ex-wife, huh? Before they got divorced. She was around the house. She was *there*, and she fuckin' hated him. Don't you think if there had been some kind of molestation bullshit going on, she would have come forward and ratted him out by now?

There was nothing...suspicious...or perverted...going on. It was honestly laughably innocent. Fuckin' Disney wouldn't have censored us, dude. What was going on was...I mean, we were having, like, *business* meetings, basically. Talking about the Manor, how to improve it. Doing video calls with Betty from her dorm room. Talking about horror and what we liked about it and what we didn't. Usually we watched a movie or two in his living room. Gnarly shit like *Hostel* and *Cannibal Holocaust* and *Martyrs*. Anything we could use for inspiration. Anything that would help us make the most extreme, scariest haunt anybody's ever dared enter.

Gus talked a lot about other haunts. How they were all too cowardly to take things to the next level. Well he wasn't no coward, and neither were we. What would we need to do to step it up? We would need to do things nobody else was doing. We would need to start touching people. We would need to physically lay our hands on them. Yes to all that, but also? We would need to really hurt them.

We would need to make them fear for their lives.

He told us about how he met Betty, how he'd tested things on her a few months before the rest of us got involved. How he'd tied her up, ripped her shirt, made her think he was cutting her open with a chainsaw. How she'd screamed until her throat was so raw she could barely talk. It got so extreme the neighbors called the cops and it became this whole thing. But instead of pressing charges or suing him, the girl became the Manor's new social media person.

The point being, there was something powerful about fear. It unlocked something in your brain that you didn't know existed, and nine times out of ten you found yourself grateful to the person responsible for its undoing.

He also viewed the cops showing up as a positive. You know how much press that gave him? It was the talk of the town, man. Fuckin' everybody was gossiping about the evil things going on at Gus McKinley's house. It was brilliant. *Gus* was brilliant. He knew exactly what he was doing. After everything that had happened with Betty and the cops, he knew his grand opening that October couldn't be tame. He had to lean into the rumors. The new and improved McKinley Manor had to be legitimately fucking scary.

BETTY ROCKSTEADY

The goal, basically, was to make H.H. Holmes look like child's play.

DEBORAH KEATON

Gus didn't start talking about hypnosis until near the end of our marriage. I'm not saying he wasn't actively researching it, but it wasn't like he ever shared anything with me. Not until those last couple months that we were together, before I made the decision to take our son and start a new life somewhere far away from Gus and his weirdo haunted house bullshit.

This happened during one of the rare times we all had dinner together. Usually he ate alone in his office, scrolling Facebook. But I hounded his ass and told him Charlie was beginning to forget he had a dad. So he came out and sat at the kitchen table with us. His eyes were…crazy, like he hadn't slept in days. He always looked like that, leading up to a haunt. By then he was doing them every weekend. Not exclusively in October like most of these attractions, but all year. I'd learned to spend Saturday nights at my mother's house. I wanted nothing to do with the haunted house anymore—it had become something I found repulsive and burdensome, and…and *terrifying*. Terrifying not because the haunts were scary, you understand, but because *Gus* was scary.

I made the mistake of asking what he'd been up to on the computer. He told me he was practicing. "Practicing what?" I asked, and he answered, matter-of-factly, "Hypnotism." I remember making him repeat himself, because I was sure I'd misheard him. But I hadn't.

I asked him, you know, *why*. He said it helped him with the haunts. How he could deceive people into thinking one thing was happening when another thing was the truth. He said he could make someone sit in a kid's swimming pool, like one of those tiny inflatable ones, and convince them that there was a great white shark swimming nearby, and they'd start freaking out, begging for rescue.

He said he'd been practicing hypnosis since he was a little kid, and it wasn't until the Manor opened that he realized the reason why. It was an incredible feeling, he told me, to have complete and total control over another human being. To make them believe anything he wanted them to believe. To hack their minds and take over.

HOWIE MCKINLEY

He used to bring home books from the library about all that nonsense. He was deeply interested in learning everything there was to know about those MKUltra experiments. I always told him he was taking that stuff too far, but he told me he was only curious about it all, that it didn't matter if it wasn't real, he still wanted to learn about it. I suspect he was lying to me back then, about not buying into it all. I should have forced him to return the library books and banned him from reading such sinful material. Lord knows his momma would've, if she'd been around to witness such leisurely activity in our household. Sometimes he'd look at me, and talk in such a peculiar manner, that I wondered if he was trying to do something to me, something out of one of his hypnosis books. Did it ever work? Did he ever…*hypnotize* me? Well, sir, I like to believe the answer is no—however, after doing a little studying into the topic on my own, I've come to conclude that if I *had* been hypnotized, I would not have any recollection of it. So I guess the whole thing is a crapshoot, ain't it?

RYAN BRADLEY, *former haunt participant*

I was tied to a table. Like the ones they make you sit back in at the dentist. I couldn't move. Not my arms, my legs. I was strapped. The only thing I could do was turn my head this way and that to look at the fucked-up shit they were doing to me. There were three of them. They all had pillowcases over their heads. Only their eyes were exposed. I was wearing a yellow duck outfit and they'd ripped one of the sleeves off already. Now I could see why. One of the guys was holding this old, rusty knife and he started pressing the tip against my flesh. I thought it was a prop until I felt how sharp it actually was, and then blood—*my* blood—started streaming out of me. Not a lot, but if you want my opinion even a *little bit* of blood coming out of your body is still too much fucking blood. It didn't stop there. One of them—they all looked the same wearing those masks—one of them, they had a syringe. Filled with what, I have no idea. Whatever it was, they injected it into my arm. Into my vein. "*Uh oh*," they said, all of them giggling like high schoolers, "*you're in for it now.*"

BETTY ROCKSTEADY

I let him hypnotize me a few times over the phone. Sure, why not? I'm up for anything at least once. He had me close my eyes and not say anything. Told me to lay there and listen. I thought it was cool. Pretty fucking kinky, honestly. The shit he would say—*goddamn*.

ZACH CHAPMAN

He tried to teach me some of his tricks. Like, his brainwashing tricks. I didn't have the patience for 'em, though. My wife suspects I got undiagnosed ADHD or something. I don't know anything about that but maybe it's not too farfetched. Like I got the cash to see a doctor. You know what kinda jobs they give ex-convicts? Not ones that can pay for health insurance, that's for damn sure. Looking back now, I'm still not positive I fully bought into the mind-control stuff. Gus was cool and all, but he was also a little, uh, whacky. He said a lot of shit that didn't make the most sense. He told us he could brainwash anyone he wanted. If that were really true, then how do I know he didn't brainwash *me*, right? Or any of us. Or how about all the haters? Why didn't he brainwash everybody into loving him? Would have saved us a lot of trouble. Shit, man, you think about it that way—why didn't he brainwash the cops into not arresting me? Why didn't he *save me*? Gus couldn't brainwash anybody. He liked to mess around. He liked to pretend.

ELLIE ROY, *former haunt participant*

Everywhere I turned, dismembered limbs swung in my face. They were hanging from chains connected to the ceiling. Dripping blood. *Fake* blood, I tried to remind myself. Just as the limbs were fake. Made of rubber. Only they didn't feel like rubber. Not there. Not then. They were too heavy. They were too *warm*. Something wasn't right, and it hadn't been right since I made it to the Manor, since I stepped foot on the property, since I was shoved into the shed. It was a cursed place. A rotten place. A haunted place. I should have never ignored the internal alarm that ignited as we arrived. *Stop being a baby*, I'd told myself—but why? Why had I told myself that? What was wrong with being a baby? Babies understood there wasn't a difference between the rational and irrational. Babies understood they didn't need to justify why something was scary. Horror doesn't care about logic. It doesn't care about realism. Its only job is to frighten you, and it will do whatever it takes to finish the job.

JOHN BALTISBERGER

The first time I went out there, back when he had that woman tied up and chainsawed her with a popsicle, there was no contract or waiver in place to the best of my knowledge. That didn't come until later, once he'd worked out a few kinks and figured out exactly what he was trying to accomplish. He never showed it to me and I never asked to see it. I'd heard rumors of its page length but I was never too interested in investigating it. What business does a cop have with contracts? That's lawyer business, far as I'm concerned. I wouldn't know the first thing about no contract.

BETTY ROCKSTEADY

The contract was meant to be a joke—until it wasn't, and it saved his ass after that stupid bitch drowned herself. But before then, you know, it was just a way to scare people. Part of his hypnosis magic. Start exhausting the mind early, make them believe all this crazy shit is in store for them. Not many people realize this, but I was actually the one who came up with most of the contract. I got super high one day and wrote the funniest possible shit I could think of, and people *ate it up*.

Let's see…I'm trying to think of a couple examples. I'm not sure where a saved copy of the contract might be, it's been so long since I needed it. But…oh yeah. [*Laughs.*] I remember it saying something about the chances being high that participants would experience carbon monoxide poisoning. Oh and that participants understand that the potentiality of whiplash, stroke, brain aneurysm, death, etc. Literally you see a contract that says you might die, and you sign it? Wild shit, right?

Okay, I'm remembering this more. What else did it say? [*Laughs.*] Okay, yeah, it's coming back. One of the sections warned participants that they may be, uh, *crushed* in a pit of "various objects." There were a lot of disclaimers that they might get crushed during their tour. *Crushed!* So vague and cartoonish! At one point in the contract there's a reference to *quicksand*, for crying out loud. I thought for sure people would read that and go, "Oh, this is clearly a joke."

But, at the same time, I did add in some real shit, to blend in with the obviously fake threats. Such as Gus using MKUltra on people. All that hypnosis stuff, he was really doing that during the tours. It might be hard to pick up on while watching some of the streams, but if you go back to a few of them with this in mind, you'll start noticing what I'm talking about, I guarantee it.

We also had to have stuff in the contracts making participants guarantee they were sober and had proper health insurance. Plus, they had to sign that they weren't members of any undercover sting operations designed to take down Gus and the Manor. I don't mean, like, the fuckin' cops or anything. But there *were* hate groups out there. People who didn't understand what the Manor was all about, and wanted to see it die. SJWs, soy boys, whatever you want to call 'em. They were all the same spineless pussies. We did catch the occasional mole trying to infiltrate the haunt. We didn't *do* anything to them, or anything. Usually Gus made them get off his property, and we'd post their photos on social media and shame them for being party poopers. They'd go home with their tail between their legs, crying to their mommies and daddies, and usually that was all it took.

ZACH CHAPMAN

The contract got me real fuckin' excited when Gus first showed it to us. I thought, holy shit, are we really gonna be able to do this to people? But nah. He was quick to lower my expectations. Some of the stuff, yes, we would be trying out, but the majority of it was just another method of brainwashing. Using their imaginations as a weapon against them. It was still kinda cool, I suppose. In theory, at least. In reality, though? Dude. Sitting there at the park as Gus went over all hundred or whatever pages of a contract with them, weekend after weekend? Boring as piss, man. Plus we had to stand there the whole time with those pillowcases over our heads. In fucking *Texas*. What the hell was he thinking?

MIGUEL MYERS

The contract was a strange thing. Every haunt worth their salt is going to make you sign a waiver if you want to participate, but I think this might've been the first instance I'd ever known about of turning the *contract itself* into part of the haunt. I believe the rumored page count was in the triple digits, and Gus would spend *hours* going over it with each participant at the beginning of the haunt. Literal hours of telling these people how they might get injured or die after they signed on the dotted line. In that way, the contract became one of the scares. Easily one of the most creative, low-budget tricks I've come across in all of my days as a professional haunter. I would never claim to be a fan of McKinley Manor, but I'm also not stubborn enough to admit when something impresses me. I'm still curious how it helped him, legally, since it was full of red flags that clearly could have never realistically been used in a court of law, yet…it *did* seem to benefit him in more ways than one, didn't it? Very, very strange. But that was Gus McKinley in a nutshell, wasn't it? A very, very strange man doing very, very strange things.

DEBORAH KEATON

The prize money wasn't something he introduced until after our divorce. Fifty thousand dollars? Not on his life. Friends asked me about it, and I told them all the same thing: it was a big, fat lie. Nobody would ever win that. He'd make sure of it.

BETTY ROCKSTEADY

I saw pics of the cash. It was definitely real. Gus kept it hidden on his property. I won't say where. I also won't say what happened to it. But he did post pictures of himself with the money in our Facebook group. Thick stacks of green. It's funny, the shit people try to say is fake. It doesn't matter if you show them photographic evidence or not. Once someone wants to believe in a conspiracy, there's no talking them out of it. There was no convincing those hater groups that Gus wasn't anything but the monster they'd made up their minds that he was. They didn't *want* him to be a good person. They needed someone to hate, and for whatever reason they'd decided he was the perfect target.

ZACH CHAPMAN

I never saw cash like that floating around. None of us did, I don't think. He posted a few pics of himself holding it. Not sure if he'd photoshopped those or what. If it *was* real, it was a good thing he didn't let slip where it was stashed. Don't forget how he recruited most of us. We were thieves, dawg. That fifty-thou would've been snatched like *that*.

JOHN BALTISBERGER

Quite a hefty sum for letting a guy scare you in his back yard. Some people believe the money never existed, but I don't know what they base these theories on. Far as I'm concerned, a man's word is a man's word. He might've struck me as a *weird* fella, but he never came across as *dishonest*. No, sir, not with me.

CHRISTINE ADDAMS

The man worked at Walmart. He didn't have fifty dollars, much less fifty *thousand*. Anyone who believed the prize money was real ought've been tested for some vitamin deficiency or something. Only thing I can think of that'd excuse being *that* gullible.

HOWIE MCKINLEY

I don't think it's a father's business to discuss his family's financial situation with strangers.

MIGUEL MYERS

Everybody likes to bring up the photographic evidence Gus provided of the fifty-thousand-dollar prize money. I would encourage people to zoom in on those photos and take a closer inspection at the money he's holding. Keen observers will notice the words "MOTION PICTURE" printed across the edges of the bills. It's prop money. [*Laughs.*] He probably purchased it in bulk either online or at his local Party City.

ZACH CHAPMAN

You gotta understand, the way shit evolved with the Manor, it wasn't overnight. There was a lot of trial and error. As far back as when those first couple videos took off on YouTube, we were still trying to, like, *figure out* the process, you know? That was the beauty of the whole thing. No haunt was identical to the last. We were always improvising, brainstorming. It was the most creative outlet any of us had ever been gifted.

There was a lot of experimentation when it came to the touching. We started small and gradually increased our limits. First we would grab people, maybe give them a squeeze. The first time I punched someone, it wasn't something that we'd planned. This fucking guy, he thought it would be funny to step on my foot. This went against the rules of any extreme haunt that allowed physical contact. The actors could touch *you*, but you were *not* allowed to touch the actors back. You know. Like a fuckin' lap dance. Except way more violent. But no. What did he do? Nearly broke my goddamn toes. So I slugged him in the gut as hard as I could. He doubled over, out of breath, then fell down. Started freaking out like I'd overreacted. I leaned into it. I embraced it. I asked him where he thought he was. I said, "Do you think you're going to make it out of here alive?" and I started kicking him in the ribs over and over until Gus had to drag me off him. Later that night, the same dude gave the Manor a five-star Google business review. "Most extreme haunt I've ever been through," the review said. "McKinley Manor is the real deal."

After that, Gus started getting on our asses if we *didn't* rough folks up.

CHRISTINE ADDAMS

I watched a few clips on his YouTube page. Couldn't finish any of them, though. What normal person could? I was sick seeing those. Physically sick. Knowing that was going on across from my house, and nobody was doing anything about it? Someone oughta give me an award for not burning down that pervert's home while he was still alive. Don't think the idea didn't cross my mind once or twice. Or maybe, instead of an award, I should be punished for denying the Manor an early demise.

HOWIE MCKINLEY

One Thanksgiving, Gus insisted on showing me some clips from his haunted house that he'd saved on his cell phone. He didn't bring them up until after I'd taken a couple bites of turkey. I could tell by the look on his face that the whole point of having me watch these videos *right then* was to gross me out, just as he used to do when he was a boy. That was the only time I ever saw any footage. I never had any desire to before then, and you can imagine I had no desire to afterward, either. It wasn't my thing. Horror, that is. I always preferred westerns, personally. *Bonanza*, now that's what I consider high-quality entertainment.

JOHN BALTISBERGER

Barb sent me a few videos once, after he started becoming a little bit of an internet celebrity. I never had the stomach to watch them, tell you the truth. Horror movies and other sicko stuff like that. It was never for me. And, besides, I reckoned I'd done experienced my fair share of McKinley Manor that day I busted open his shed door. There was no reason to further subject myself to that kinda silliness.

MIGUEL MYERS

Every haunted house utilizes a safe word. It's standard practice. To not do so is unprofessional and tacky. Even other extreme venues give out safe words. Yeah, they might force you to eat vomit, but if you tell them you want to stop, they'll stop. For whatever reason, that was something Gus could never get on board with. That was only one of many reasons McKinley Manor never earned our respect. The whole setup felt like a child playing with a loaded handgun. It was embarrassing.

BETTY ROCKSTEADY

Safe words. Safe spaces. That was all cowardly bullshit. We weren't like the other haunted houses. We didn't care about your feelings. We didn't care if you were offended. We *wanted* to offend you. We were the real fucking deal. It wasn't like we kept that fact a secret, you know? You knew right from the start, you don't get a safe word. We didn't believe in them. You don't like it? Then don't do the fucking haunt, dipshit. What was so complicated about that?

ZACH CHAPMAN

You wanna hear something kinda hilarious, but also a little screwed up? At one point, we *did* try out a safe word. Nobody seems to know about it, though. We never announced it or made the knowledge public, or anything. But for a couple haunts we started telling participants—before the streaming started—that, at any point they no longer felt safe and wanted the tour to abruptly end, all they had to do was shout the n-word. Right into the camera, for the whole world to see forever. Their friends, their loved ones, their future employers. Scream the n-word as loud as you can. Now, I'm not saying the real word here because I'm on parole still and I don't quite understand how that shit works, but you know what I mean. I'm not afraid to say the word. It's important to me for your readers to understand that I'm not a snowflake. But anyway, nobody ever took us up on it. Peculiar, ain't it? Naturally Gus grew bored with that idea after a few weeks since it wasn't going anywhere, and we went back to not having one at all—but, like, c'mon, it wasn't like people still couldn't quit, if they wanted to. *Most* people tapped out. We just took our time putting on the brakes, is all. Only a rare few we had to pull out ourselves, from judgement calls on their personal health and safety.

JOHN BALTISBERGER

I don't know much about haunted houses. I've heard some have safe words and some don't. I know Gus didn't. Some people found that controversial. Personally, the way I figure it, if you're dumb enough to sign a contract giving a stranger permission to do all types of ungodly activities to your mind and body, there's not much good a safe word's gonna do. You're well past that point. But again, what do I know? I wouldn't have signed up if someone paid me. My momma didn't raise no ignoramus.

CHRISTINE ADDAMS

Gus was a pervert, plain and simple. Torturing people made him come. That was the whole point of this shit. It was why he didn't charge money, why the process was the way it was. You ever see the videos of him at the park, before he takes his "victims" back to his house? After he forces them to do those weird exercises, he sprays their faces with paint—usually while moaning. I'm no psychoanalyst or whatever you'd call it, but I think it's clear what that paint was supposed to symbolize. [*Long pause.*] Male ejaculation.

JOHN BALTISBERGER

I heard all the conspiracy theories about Gus. You got any idea how many people called up the station to tell us some insane secret about what was going on over there? Gus was forming a cult. Gus was killing and replacing his haunted house contestants with androids in an attempt to take over the world. Gus was streaming everything on the dark web and letting foreign countries gamble on how long people would last before giving up. Gus was a rapist. Gus was a murderer. Gus was a con man. Gus was a dog man. That one was my favorite—the dog man theory. Not exactly a werewolf, but close. A man who changes into a dog. [*Laughs.*] You ever hear of such a crazy thing before? That was why he wanted everybody to bring dog food. Because he was eating it. Did I believe any of it? Not a lick. Do I think Gus had secrets? What man doesn't? More important question is what business was it of anyone's? Would you want someone knowing *your* secrets and gossiping all around town with every Tom, Dick, and Harry? I don't think so.

ZACH CHAPMAN

Some of those accusations, you know, they weren't, like…*totally* off base, or anything. Like the gambling? Okay, so the whole livestreaming to Thailand shit was cartoon talk, but there *was* an aspect of gambling going on at the haunt. Maybe not with Gus specifically, but amongst actors? You bet your ass we were placing bets. We had this whole thing going, every tour we'd each throw five or ten bucks into a pot, and whichever actor got the mark to give up first got to keep the cash. This was back when the Manor was in its prime, and we had like a dozen actors volunteering. A lot of them drifted away for one reason or another. Some moved, or went to college, or got jobs, or started families—real normie shit. I'm not judging. Look at me, I got a regular job, I got a family. It only took getting incarcerated for that to happen.

BETTY ROCKSTEADY

Okay, here *is* a secret. All those conspiracy theories people put out there about Gus? He loved them. He thought they were hilarious, and so did I. The wild shit people would make up about him. It never ceased to amuse us. We'd joke about it on the phone all the time. Whatever new thing the haters were claiming about him. The one that made us laugh the most, though, was the idea that he was streaming everything to places like Russia and the Philippines. He used to say to me, "Who the hell do I know from the Philippines, Betty? I'm a Texas boy." Everybody thought he was getting secretly rich from underground gambling rings on the dark web. That always cracked me up. Gus barely understood how to help moderate the Facebook group. You think he knew jack shit about the dark web?

JOHN BALTISBERGER

I was probably one of the last to hear about the petition. I think Barb forwarded me the link. It seemed silly to me. How did the town react? They didn't. At least not to my knowledge. It wasn't like we had ourselves a town hall meeting about it or anything. [*Laughs.*] Honestly, I think most of the people worked up about the whole thing weren't actually residents of Pork Basket. I doubt most of them were even Texans, if you want me to shoot it to you straight. You know how folks on the internet can get. They're, uh, you know—*sensitive*. Besides, when the hell has a petition ever done anything? You know how many petitions I've seen in my life? You know how many of them ever made the slightest impact? Nada. Zippo.

DEBORAH KEATON

I knew the Manor had gotten extreme and disgusting, but I'm not sure I understood *how* extreme until the petition went live. It prompted me to watch some of the videos I'd been avoiding. They made me sad, you know? To see someone I once loved taking such pleasure in waterboarding people, in slapping and kicking them. The spirit of those old boo haunts we used to do together was long dead. In its place was this new, sick...*thing* that I couldn't understand. I didn't *want* to understand it, either. Back before I left—this was probably the last week we lived together as a married couple—I'd confronted him about the direction things were heading. The way he'd become completely and totally obsessed with the Manor. He tried to blame it on PTSD he'd gotten from the Marines. He told me the only time the voices in his head calmed down was when he was doing a haunt. It's possible what he said was the truth. Either way, it wasn't enough to convince me to stay. He could have sought therapy. Instead he chose to create a sicko torture chamber in our back yard. So yeah. I signed the petition. I moved on with my life. I was already out of the house by then. Out of the *state*. This was no longer my problem. *Gus* was no longer my problem. I had a son to raise.

CHRISTINE ADDAMS

I was thrilled when I saw it online. I forget where, exactly. Someone might've posted it in the Pork Basket community Facebook group. It was a petition demanding for the immediate closure of McKinley Manor. Gus was an evil man, the petition said, and he had to be stopped at all costs.

Looking back, though, I don't know what good it did. All it ended up doing was giving him a lot of free advertisement. If I didn't know any better, I'd say he started the petition himself.

[*Pauses.*]
[*Laughs.*]
That sneaky motherfucker.

BETTY ROCKSTEADY

Shit, you know, I guess you're getting all the juicy gossip out of me today. Let's talk about the petition. You ever wonder who started it? Like, who, exactly went through all the trouble of writing it up and spreading it around the internet? Why don't you think about who would have benefited the most from it? We went fuckin' viral. Like, they were talking about us *on the fucking news*. You think we were mad about that? You think Gus was upset? We were thrilled. Things couldn't have been more exciting. Of *course* we started the petition. And you idiots ate it up like candy. As Gus used to say: hook, line, and sinker, baby.

MIGUEL MYERS

I guess, to conclude our conversation, I would like to leave your readers with a few things to think about.

Haunted house attractions are designed to entertain people. Sometimes they go too far, sometimes they don't go far enough. Ask a dozen different people who go through the same haunt and they'll all have different criticisms. McKinley Manor was not the first extreme haunt to allow touching. Many have done it before them, and many have done it after them. That, itself, was not a novelty. Anyone who claims McKinley Manor was problematic due to that alone is simply uneducated on how haunts work.

But what *does* align McKinley Manor into problematic territory has to do with the way its owner utilized deceit. The way it played into its own questionable advertising. The simple fact is: McKinley Manor was never the type of haunted house it claimed to be. For one thing, you never actually entered a house. The majority of the haunt took place in his back yard. Sometimes you'd get taken into a shed, but that was about it. The attraction also advertised several misleading scares. There were no live insects on the property—at least none intended for the haunt. There was no "two-mile zipline" you were forced onto. There was no underground lagoon, and there certainly weren't any alligators. These were all false promises.

Instead, when one attended Gus McKinley's haunt, you would find something far more disappointing. You would be forced to mow his lawn and perform standard gym class exercises. Nobody attends a haunted house hoping to spend half the day doing sit-ups in the sun, yet that is what happened there more often than not. You would be stuffed into a barrel and waterboarded by a man wearing a pillowcase over his head. You would be physically punched and kicked in the back of a van by unsupervised teenagers. There was no true emphasis on *spookiness*. There was nothing here that played into the spirit of traditional haunts. There was just…*nihilism*.

And that would have been perfectly acceptable, had that been the type of experience Gus advertised. Instead, he misled folks into expecting something far more creative and fulfilling. And, due to his rabid fanbase's help with mass-reporting any video or article that exposed McKinley Manor for what it really was, Google's search results for the attraction also consistently deceived newcomers. Before the killings, whenever you searched McKinley Manor, the top page on Google provided only videos created *by* Gus. Which meant, whenever someone first heard about the Manor and tried to learn more, the initial burst of information available would be—essentially—propaganda. That's how you'd get so many people signing up and flying in from all over the country—all over the *world*, reportedly. People losing money not just from travel expenses but also hotel fees, not to mention whatever income they might've missed requesting the time off from their jobs. All because of why? For the chance to experience what was supposed to be the world's greatest haunted house? For the opportunity to win fifty-thousand dollars that never existed in the first place?

Meanwhile, what was *really* happening? They were being duped. They were being humiliated for everybody in the McKinley Manor Facebook group. It was all part of the show, so they could be laughed at and ridiculed as Gus sprayed their faces with a hose until they couldn't take it any longer. Until they either tapped out or drowned.

That, to me, is what was so unethical about McKinley Manor. Not that Gus tortured people, but the fact that he misrepresented himself. If he'd only been honest, so much could have been different.

So many lives could have been saved.

Chapter Two

The Killing of Jessica Henderson

TREVOR HENDERSON, *brother of Jessica Henderson*

When Jessica died, she was only twenty-two. I was seventeen. It's crazy to think that I'm now older than her, you know what I mean? She'll never *not* be twenty-two. No more, no less. Do you understand how hard that is to truly comprehend?

When I hit my twenty-second birthday in here, I lost my mind. I'm usually cool and collected. I don't do anything to anybody. I mind my own business. That's how you survive in a place like this. But not that day. I went nuts. Guards had to restrain me and everything. Spent the whole day in solitary, which had maybe been my goal the whole time, if you really want to analyze it. Nobody wants to mourn in front of others. That's a private act.

When I was a kid, Jessica had been my whole world. I thought she was the coolest. She wasn't like other big sisters. Sure, she teased me the normal amount any older sibling does, but she wasn't, like, *embarrassed* to hang out with me, or anything. If she was going somewhere, and I asked to tag along, there was never any hesitation. She'd say hell yeah, Trevor, go get your shoes on.

And you'd think that would have changed once she started dating—especially when she started dating Andrew, but you'd be wrong. It certainly caused a bit of strife sometimes. It wasn't like Andrew knew how to keep his mouth shut when he was annoyed about something. And this was a guy who was always annoyed about everything. But she didn't seem to care. He might've been able to boss her around on most other things and get his way, except when it came to me. If you crossed me, you were on her shit list. Andrew found this out early on in their relationship. Still, though. I could tell how he really felt about me. Anyone could. I was a nuisance. I was *in the way*.

ANDREW HILBERT, *ex-boyfriend of Jessica Henderson*

Jessica was all fucked up. I know it might not be, uh, *PC* or whatever to say that, but it's the truth. She wasn't no angel. She wasn't no saint. She wasn't none of that shit. You think she broke up with me? You're out of your goddamn mind. How about *I* broke up with *her*? Yeah, that's right. Did I just blow your mind? Don't get me wrong, man. It sucks that she died and all. But I get sick and tired of hearing everybody talk about her like she was some perfect girl gift-wrapped from heaven. Jessica wasn't perfect. I could tell you stories, oh man, you got no idea. Stories that'd make you absolutely disgusted. But I'm not about to do that. I was raised proper, you know? I was taught not to speak ill of the dead. But seriously, though? Look, I'm sorry, but Jessica was a fucking bitch.

TREVOR HENDERSON

Mom and Dad encouraged me to join Jessica whenever she went out. I think they thought if I was around, then she couldn't get into trouble. She was too responsible to let her guard down with me there, is what they probably assumed. Of course, that wasn't exactly *true*. I witnessed her do things I swore never to tell. I've seen my sister high, I've seen her drunk, I've seen her crying and I've seen her laughing like nobody's ever seen her laugh before.

I've even seen her having sex.

I wish I could say by accident, but what's the point in lying when the rest of your future's already cemented in place by the government?

And besides, it's not like I'm trying to confess to having been, uh, sexually attracted to my sister, or anything. I'm not, like, a pervert or anything. No more than anyone else, at least.

I was sixteen and I was sleeping over at the new

apartment Jessica and Andrew had moved into together. It was a studio, which meant there was only one bedroom, so I was sleeping out in the living room. They didn't have any furniture yet. Blankets and pillows on the floor and that was about it. I didn't mind. Teenagers have spines made of steel. If anything, it was good practice for prison cots.

I fell asleep watching some movie, I don't know what, but I woke up sometime in the middle of the night needing to pee. Halfway to the bathroom is when I heard them. There were…noises. Heavy breathing. I knew what they were doing, and I knew I should've peed and went back to sleep. But I was sixteen, man. At that age, some stuff is just…beyond your control, you know?

I opened the door. Only a little bit. Enough to peek through. And I saw them. Nobody was covered up. Not in the summer — not in Texas.

They were naked. He was on top of her. It looked…*rough*. In that moment, I remember having a hard time understanding how it could've been pleasurable for either of 'em. Unfortunately, the door made a creaking noise, and they caught me lookin'. It wasn't like I was trying to spy on them. I just wanted to see. Only for a second. I had to. I couldn't *not*. Andrew, though, he freaked out. Started saying things like I was jacking off. But I wasn't. They saw I had a hard-on in my underwear and assumed the worst. But the honest truth is, I still had to pee. [*Laughs.*] That's all it was, I swear.

Andrew, he wanted to tear my head off. And he might've, if Jessica hadn't been there to stop him. I have to say, though, even Jessica wasn't on my side that night, and afterward the invitations to sleep over started appearing less and less frequently.

ANDREW HILBERT

If that little creep wasn't masturbating, then tell me why his hand was down his pants when we caught him? Better yet, explain the cum stain on his tighty whites. [*Laughs.*] You want my opinion? I'll tell you what I've told everybody who's ever asked about it. Little ol' Trevor was in love with my Jess. Like, *in love* in love. I'm talkin'…fuckin' *Games of Thrones*, man. Seriously. Like, homepage-of-Pornhub shit. What I'm saying is, he wanted to fuck his sister, all right? And I was the only one who saw through him. Saw him for who he was.

TREVOR HENDERSON

My sister…

My sister, she…

The thing you need to—the thing *everybody* needs to understand about my sister is, she never did anything to anybody. She was the nicest person I've ever known. And what did she get in return? Dead. She got herself *killed*.

All because of Gus goddamn McKinley.

Okay, to be fair, it wasn't entirely Gus's fault.

It was everybody who worked for Gus, too.

Plus…there was Jessica's ex. Have you talked to Andrew yet? I wouldn't recommend it. I've smelled better breath coming out of a donkey's ass.

You try talking to him and he'll act like he's innocent in the whole thing, but the truth is she would have never gone to the Manor if not for him.

Without him in her life, I think it's safe to say my sister would be alive right now.

But that's not the situation we find ourselves in, is it?

Okay. Sorry. I guess this stuff still makes me crazy emotional. The more I talk about it all, the harder it gets to think straight. You asked about how she used to be, back when she was alive. Her hobbies? She watched a lot of movies, I guess. Old movies. Black and white stuff. You ever see *Paper Moon*? That was one of her favorites. Her and I watched it a thousand times together. This dude and his daughter driving around during the Great Depression scamming people. Man, I haven't seen that movie in forever. I'd kill for the guards to play it here. Obviously they won't, given the content, but still. That'd be perfect. Just thinking about *Paper Moon* right now is enough to make me want to cry. You never really stop missing someone, you know? They never leave your life. Not really.

Besides movies…well, she loved dogs, of course. Dachshunds, specifically. The one and only tattoo she ever got was a paw print of the family wiener. Bosco was his name. He died a few years before she did. Found a chicken bone in the trash and that was all it took. One day you have a dog and then one day you don't. One day you have a sister and then one day you don't. One day you have a future and then one day you're serving multiple life sentences in a maximum-security state penitentiary. Isn't life funny that way?

ANDREW HILBERT

The first time I fucked Jessica, she let me come on her face. That's how I knew she was special. Ain't no girl ever let me do something like that before. I told myself, *Don't lose this one*, but that was before I realized she was nuts—which seems to be my track records with girls. Crazy bitches. I can't help it, though. Crazy pussy beats out normal pussy any day of the week. They just ain't built for long-lasting, uh, stable relationships, is the thing.

TREVOR HENDERSON

Andrew's the one who told her about Gus. Told both of us about him, actually. I was at their apartment when he brought it up. I remember the day perfectly. It's so clear that sometimes, when I can't sleep, I transport myself from my cell to that afternoon and try my hardest to alter the chain of events. But it doesn't matter what I do. I can't change the past. Nor the future, if you want to get down to it. Not where I am, at least. Lifers don't have much hope left, you know? All we can do is sit around and wait to die. What else is there, right?

Well, besides this book you're writing. This is something *new*. Something *different*. Will it *change* anything, though? I remain doubtful. Anybody going into this will have already made up their minds on what transpired all those years ago. Either you already believe me or you don't.

Sorry. There I go getting worked up again. Notice that tends to happen whenever I start talking about Andrew. But I gotta talk about him, don't I? He's the whole fucking reason Jessica ever found out about Gus. I don't know who told *him* about Gus, though. Maybe he discovered him on his own. There was that Netflix documentary about haunters. It'd come out around then, if I remember correctly. Or maybe he found one of his videos on YouTube or Reddit. Either way, this is how it happened:

Jessica and I are playing *Mario Kart* on her Wii. She's kicking my ass, like she always did. We have plans to make a frozen pizza soon and watch *New Girl*. Back then, I would have been embarrassed to admit how much I liked that show, but I don't see the point in being embarrassed about something like that now. I'll admit it fully, and on the record. *New Girl* is hilarious. Fucking Schmidt, are you serious? C'mon, bro. Don't even try to pretend like you don't also love *New Girl*.

But anyway. We're playing *Mario Kart*, and Andrew's

sitting at the kitchen counter screwing around on his laptop. Then, suddenly, he starts laughing and saying things like, "Oooh, shit," and, "Yooo, what the fuck!" You can only ignore somebody like that so long before they get so loud you can't think straight. Finally Jessica asks Andrew what he's looking at, and he makes us pause our game and join him in the kitchen. He already has one of the videos queued up for us.

"Y'all know about this fuckin' guy?" he asks us. "He's a fuckin' nutjob."

Then he clicks PLAY, and the video we watch is unlike any horror movie I've ever seen. It feels *real*. It feels *dangerous*. I immediately hate it, and so does Jessica. Only Andrew seems to find the humor in what we're watching.

Do I really need to get into details here? I know Gus's YouTube channel got taken down after…you know, but I'm sure if you really want to watch his shit, someone's uploaded them somewhere, like, on the dark web or something, I don't know.

It wasn't a full-length haunt. More of a clip show of several haunts. Like a highlight reel. A *best-of*. I remember there was some heavy metal song overlapping it that I sincerely doubt Gus had secured the rights to use. I'm surprised that itself wasn't enough to get the video flagged. Not to mention the graphic violence on display.

Anyone interested in Gus McKinley has probably already seen the video, to be honest. It was the big one that went viral. Clips of people covered in blood. People screaming. Blindfolded and hogtied. Just…you know. Stuff like that.

[*Pauses.*]

I don't really want to talk about the videos. I don't like thinking about them. All this does is gets me all worked up, and sure, that might be what you're hoping to accomplish, but I want no part in it if that's the case.

ANDREW HILBERT

Man, those videos were a fuckin' riot. It took some time but I eventually got through every last one of 'em. Some real gnarly shit, man. Especially those early ones. Motherfuckers tied up in bathtubs vomiting in buckets and being forced to drink it all back up. Full-on slapping them across the face and cutting their hair. Plus the waterboarding, which I guess is kinda fucked up to think about now, but ain't that what they advertised would happen, anyway? It wasn't like the videos were private or anything, right?

I did haunted houses and shit when I was a kid. We all did. Every October. It was fun. Not like *scary* or anything, but it was fun. We sure as hell never did a haunted house where they were allowed to *touch you*, much less *hit you*. That shit is crazy. When I first heard about these extreme haunts, I lost my mind. Did I want to do one? Hell nah. I ain't a fuckin' retard. Someone tries making me eat my vomit, and we're gonna have words, you know what I'm saying? But goddamn, dude, it was fun to watch *other* idiots doing it. No wonder Gus got as famous as he did. Shit was like reality TV for gore freaks.

One of my favorite videos, man, I ain't ever forgot it. There was this bitch with the biggest tits I've ever seen in my life. And the thing with McKinley Manor was, if you were doing the haunt then you were bound to get wet at *some point*, and with this bitch they didn't waste any time whatsoever in getting her drenched. I thought she was gonna fuckin' burst out of the T-shirt she was wearing, I shit you not. They must've filmed this one before everybody had to start wearing those sketchy animal onesies, come to think about it. What they did was, they forced her to lie down on this weightlifting bench, facing up toward the sky, and tied her arms back under the bench, which only seemed to make her tits *bigger*

The Last Haunt

somehow. It was, like, motherfuckin' titty rocket science or something, the way they enlarged like that. They also blindfolded her, so she had no idea what they were preparing. She was *helpless*, man. It was great.

First thing they did was, they dumped buckets of water all over her. Not just her face but her whole body. Her shirt was already wet by then, so doing it again I think was to make sure it didn't start drying. Plus, you know, she has no idea what's being poured on her. It looks like water but they're standing over her saying it's piss and blood and all this other gross shit. She can't see. She's gotta decide whether she believes what they're saying or not, and under those circumstances I'm sure you're assuming the absolute worst. Shit, who wouldn't?

So she's freaking out from the jump, and they're telling her to shut the fuck up, only they ain't saying fuck because Gus and his crew never swear, it's one of their rules. They don't swear and neither can the person being tortured. Ain't that the funniest fuckin' thing you ever heard? So instead of "shut the fuck up" I suppose it's more like "shut your mouth" and "calm down if you know what's good for ya." That kinda shit.

It don't work, though. Especially not when they pull her shirt up a little bit, exposing her stomach, and start plopping raw hamburger meat all over her flesh. This time they don't tell her what it is. They start demanding she guess. Screaming inches from her face shit like, "What do you think that is? Oh, you don't want to know! You do *not* want to know!" and she's screaming right back at them, "Get it off me! Oh god get it off me!" and she's shaking and crying but they got her tied so good she ain't going nowhere. All she's really succeeding in doing is jiggling those massive fuckin' titties for the camera, for the whole world to see. And it is a *sight*, my brother.

I'll tell you something else, too. Something I ain't been able to stop thinking about since I first saw the video. The way they had this bitch tied up, with her arms *under* the bench? You know what that looked like, from a certain angle? It didn't, like, *click* with me for the longest time, but once it did, I couldn't *not* see it that. When the camera was directly above her, aimed down at her body, I swear to god, man, it was like she didn't *have* any fuckin' arms. Like she was some fuckin', I don't know, ampu*tee* or something. Just this arm-less bitch with two mega-sized tits covered in raw meat. Screaming. Crying. It was unlike anything I'd ever seen before—or since, sadly.

And I'm not ashamed to admit that it got me hard. I don't think all of Gus's videos were meant to be, like, *erotic* or anything, and I'm not sure this particular video was meant to be like that, either, but goddamn, dude, that shit was fucking *hot*. If I ever met a girl without any arms I'd marry her in a second, and that's a fact.

Why don't they make dating apps for *that* type of shit? You ever think about that? I bet you'd make a killing.

TREVOR HENDERSON

Jessica was disgusted by the video. She told Andrew to turn it off and asked why he'd ever want to watch something like that. He chuckled and told us to stop being a bunch of pussies, which is what he always called people whenever he wasn't getting his way about something. To give him credit, he *did* stop playing them, although he wasn't done talking about Gus. Not by a long shot. He was falling down this whole rabbit hole, reading up about him and telling us everything he was finding out. That's when we learned the basics. You know, stuff like the dog food entrance fee, the one-hundred-page waiver, the lack of a safe word, and…well, and the prize money. The fifty thousand dollars.

ANDREW HILBERT

I could *not* believe nobody had made it through. Fifty thousand dollars, are you crazy? That's life-changing money. Fifty thousand dollars can solve literally any problem anybody has ever had. And all you had to do was make it through this crazy fucker's homemade torture chamber? I definitely gave some thought to doing it myself, don't get me wrong, but I was recovering from an injury at the time and knew I wouldn't be able to compete at my top physical strength. Jessica, on the other hand, ain't shit was wrong with her. She was in *great* shape. You ever see pics of her before the shit happened with the haunt? She was fit as fuck, bro.

Truth was, we were actually split up when she decided to do the haunt. Although it was *definitely* my idea and she stole it from me. This was back when we were still together. I'd offered to help train her and everything. I was the one who'd already done the homework and watched all the videos. I knew what to expect, and I could prepare her ahead of time. If we worked together on this, I was confident we could win that money. But she said no. She said I was out of my mind. Shortly after that, I had to dump her ass. It wasn't *because* of her not wanting to do the haunt, but…ya know, it didn't fuckin' help, right? It wasn't entirely *unrelated*.

TREVOR HENDERSON

I wish I knew for sure why Jessica got in contact with Gus. I have my suspicions, but I wasn't present during those conversations. This decision wasn't made until after…uh, after the incident with her and Andrew having sex with each other. After Andrew made her ban me from staying over again. We would still text once in a while, plus we'd hang out whenever she visited home, but she never talked to me about Gus McKinley again. The day Andrew showed us those videos was the only time I ever heard anything about him, and it stayed that way for several months—until my mom received the phone call that Jessica had been killed in some town we'd never heard of called Pork Basket. [*Grimaces.*] All this time, and I still can't get over that name. God, I hate Texas.

ANDREW HILBERT

What had happened was, we were living together, right? Splitting this apartment, a little studio. And we'd started falling behind on rent, and a few other debts. Now, my credit is dog shit. Always has been. You can thank my mom for that, who used to list my name on all our bills when we were growing up. I never had a chance, right? But Jessica, her credit was fine. No red marks on her record or *nothin'*.

So we got some credit cards in her name, and they got maxed out, but...like, that was the plan, wasn't it? We were going to take the credit cards, pay off our debts, maybe splurge a little bit on the latest PlayStation—I gotta have some leisure time, otherwise what's the point?—and I'd get a job and help her pay it off.

Well, she wouldn't get off my ass about the whole thing. Kept saying I'd taken advantage of her, gone behind her back, yada yada yada. Real fucking annoying about the whole thing. I'm sure you understand. I told her to eat shit, that she could figure it out herself if she wanted to treat me like that— hell, wasn't like any of it was in *my* name, after all—and I got out of there.

Couple weeks later, I find out the hard way that she'd used *my* idea of doing the haunt, and rather than take my advice and let me help train her, she'd tried doing it alone. No practice, no anything.

And look at what happened.

I tell you, I wish I could feel bad, but the truth was she'd ripped me off. I'm not saying she got what she deserved, but man, what did she expect to happen?

JOHN BALTISBERGER

It was a dark day, when I got the call about the Henderson girl. Usually it was other folks calling in about the Manor — Gus, he only contacted us prior to the haunt, never *during*, and that was to give us a heads up so nobody accidentally pulled up with their guns out. So, to get a call *from* Gus, hours after he'd already let us know he'd be doing a haunt that evening, I think Barb knew right away something had gone wrong. She told me just from the sound of his voice, she knew it was serious business.

ZACH CHAPMAN

Worst day of my fucking life, man. All these years later, and not a night passes that I don't go to sleep reliving the events. It started off like any normal haunt. Her name was Jessica Henderson. As long as I live, I'll never forget that name. How the fuck could I, right? After what we did to her. Accident or not, we still *did* it. We still killed her.

TREVOR HENDERSON

After everything was over, and we were notified, it took some time for the true horror of it all to kick in. At first we were just…*confused*. Nothing anybody said made much sense. All we were told was Jessica had taken the McKinley Manor challenge, and something had gone wrong, and she somehow…accidentally…*drowned*. Gus, of course, was already on the defense. Telling the news that he had nothing to do with what happened, that he's hosted "thousands" of haunts before and this was the first time anything had ever gone wrong. "And, besides," he said, "she signed a contract and was warned multiple times about the type of danger she was putting herself in. She knew perfectly well what *could* happen, even if it's never happened before."

JOHN BALTISBERGER

I got there five minutes before the ambulance. Someone had already pulled her out of the barrel. Gus said he'd tried resuscitating her—he was taught CPR back in his Marine days—but it was no use. She was dead. I checked her pulse and confirmed. A paramedic might've tried his own CPR on her but it was more out of politeness than anything. There was no saving her. There was no bringing her back. What was done was done.

CHRISTINE ADDAMS

I was baking a cake—red velvet, my favorite. Standing in my kitchen, washing dishes I'd dirtied from mixing the batter. I have a window overlooking the sink. Unfortunately, it gives me a perfect view of Gus's house. By coincidence, I happened to glance out of it as the girl—Jessica Henderson—escaped through the back fence gate. She was wearing one of those stupid animal onesies Gus made everybody wear, but hers was too dirty for me to figure out what species. Her wrists were bound but not her ankles. I guess she'd somehow worked herself free enough to run away. She didn't have a blindfold on, either. I'd never seen someone's eyes so wide. The poor girl was absolutely terrified. She ran down the street screaming for someone to help her, but she didn't make it very far. Two of Gus's boys, both of them wearing pillowcases, chased after her and snatched her up. Dragged her back to the house. Did I do anything to help? Maybe I should have gotten out my gun and physically put an end to it. Maybe I should've plugged his ass that first day Gus installed the sign in front of his house. A lot of things sure would be different around here if I had.

TREVOR HENDERSON

I didn't need anyone to tell me what onesie she'd been wearing. She'd owned it for years. I remember our dad having to get it custom made, since most shops didn't typically sell dachshund pajamas like that. It was a Christmas gift. I still remember how excited she got when she opened the box. Man. This stuff can really weigh you down, huh?

ZACH CHAPMAN

We were deep into the haunt when she escaped. I still don't understand how it happened—how she got loose. Could've been she wasn't restrained properly or she was some secret escape artist, I don't know, man, but either way she fucking hauled ass out of the yard—right through the gate and down the middle of Gus's street. Something like this had never happened. It was crazy. We couldn't believe it. We were all just...*livid*. How dare this chick make us look like chumps, right? That was our mindset. Gus said, "Get her back here. *Now*," and we didn't have to be told twice. Me and Trey took off after her. Caught up with her by some mailboxes. She was screaming so goddamn loud I thought her voice was going to split my skull open. It didn't help that she was also punching and kicking us as we dragged her back to the Manor. She got me a few good times right across the jaw, too, and that definitely didn't help control my temper once we got her chained up again. "Teach her a lesson," Gus told us, "teach her one she'll never forget." And, man…I don't know what else to tell you. In that moment, we were fueled solely by rage. *All* I wanted to do was teach her a lesson. I lost my mind. I forgot everything Gus had taught us about waterboarding safety protocols. It was like I'd become this…this *animal*, man. I just knew that I wanted her to fucking *pay*.

CHRISTINE ADDAMS

I called the police after they snatched her, and I told them what I'd witnessed. You know what they said? "We are already aware that a haunt is taking place tonight. There is no need to be concerned." No need to be concerned. [*Laughs.*] Goddamn, what a joke. If there was no need to be concerned, then tell me why not an hour later our whole street was lit up with emergency lights? The sound of those sirens were enough to make anyone deaf, I swear. Everybody on the block, we all came out to snoop and exchange information. See who knew what. But we already knew. Only one reason an ambulance would be coming to Gus's. Wasn't like any of us were surprised. Since that shithead started making it on the news, we were all placing bets for how long it'd take before someone died there. God's truth? Took way longer than I would have ever thought. It's a good thing there wasn't a literal bet, or else I would have lost a good chunk of change that day.

BETTY ROCKSTEADY

I was watching the stream when it happened. I knew something was wrong. The way she suddenly stopped fighting back. The way her body went…*still*. The way Gus dropped the camera. I'd never seen anybody die before.

It was scary, yeah—but also? Weirdly exciting. Not…in a sexual way or anything. I'm not a freak, okay? I'm just saying. It was weird, you know? The way my adrenaline started pumping.

I tried contacting Gus that night, but he never picked up the phone. The radio silence scared me shit-less. Everybody in the Facebook group was freaking out. Nobody could get a hold of Gus or anyone else who'd been at the haunt. I didn't hear from him until the following day, and still he was hesitant to speak about the incident.

Over the years I'd grown to know Gus, I learned when it was okay to press him on certain topics, and when I was better off dropping it altogether. This was the latter. If he wanted to talk about it, he would have been the one to engage.

JOHN BALTISBERGER

Everybody was standing around, fidgety, jumpy, nervous. They were downright *terrified,* and for good reason—Gus included. I never for a second believed any of this had been intentional. The fellas who worked for Gus might've had troubled pasts, but they seemed like good enough boys. If anything, Gus had straightened them out by providing a purpose in life. But still. Accidental or not, a girl was dead. The footage had been corrupted somehow, but after they all explained to me what happened, I thought I understood well enough. Sounded like the clearest case of manslaughter if I ever heard one. Sure, out of context it might've looked like a bonafide murder. *But*...I understood the context. The context was everything. The young woman had volunteered for this, after all. She knew what she was getting into. I know it sounds harsh to hear, but some things in life aren't sweet to the ears.

TREVOR HENDERSON

Like all of Gus's haunts, it had been livestreamed in the McKinley Manor's private Facebook group. *However*, unlike every other stream, this particular one somehow got deleted immediately after it was finished. I know the police demanded to see it, but there was supposedly nothing to show them. Something glitched, according to Gus, and he didn't know what happened to it. I wasn't a member of the group back then. I wouldn't have access to their archives for another year. I still think it's obvious what happened, though. After he realized my sister was no longer breathing, he panicked and scrubbed any video evidence of the night's event. I'm sure plenty of people in the group had managed to see the actual livestream, but it's no surprise nobody came forward. Gus's followers...that whole Facebook group, it was a cult. They followed him blindly and thought whatever he said was golden, and anybody who dared challenge his authority was a hater. "Hater" was his word, by the way. That's what he called anyone who not only criticized the Manor, but even asked *questions* about it. Shit, man, if you go back to some of his old posts following my sister's death, he called *her* a hater. And what had been her crime, exactly, huh? *Dying?*

ZACH CHAPMAN

I regret the kid I was back then. I know I've changed. I've taken classes on how to manage my anger. I've developed certain things I can say or do when I feel an episode coming on, things that can help calm me down. I guess, in a way, *that's* kind of like brainwashing, huh? Brainwashing myself to not be such a shithead. I wish more than anything I could go back to that day and do everything differently. I'm still glad I was given the opportunity to be Gus's friend, and to have been involved with the Manor, and I believe it's a real goddamn shame for it to have ended the way it did. When we were all first starting out, nobody wanted *this* to be its legacy. How fucking sad would that have been? How goddamn pathetic?

HOWIE MCKINLEY

What happened with that girl was a tragedy. It was also an accident, plain and simple. My son was a good man. He made some mistakes in his life, but he always had the purest of intentions. He would have never seriously hurt anybody on purpose. I know this with all my heart. My son was not responsible for that girl's death.

DEBORAH KEATON

After watching some of those videos on YouTube, I can't say I was surprised when I heard the news. Disappointed, yes, but not surprised. Something like that was bound to happen sooner or later. I'm just relieved Charlie and me were long gone before things truly got out of hand. In those final months of our marriage, there was a certain type of look in Gus's eyes that spooked me. Was this the man I had married? The man I thought I'd fallen in love with? If so, what did that say about me, then? How could I have let someone like that trick me into believing they weren't really a monster?

<u>TREVOR HENDERSON</u>

I didn't kill Gus, but sometimes the only thing that helps me sleep at night is knowing that motherfucker is dead.

Chapter Three

The McKinley Manor Massacre

The Last Haunt

TREVOR HENDERSON

Gus and I didn't officially meet until the following Halloween—the same day he died. After Jessica, the Manor closed and went dark on social media. I'm sure the Facebook group was still active, but only members could see what was being posted, and they weren't really interested in granting newcomers access.

Before Jessica's death—before her *murder*, the Manor had certainly attracted its fair share of publicity, both positive and negative, mostly negative, but what happened with my sister brought not just nationwide attention but *international*. For a solid two days, it was all anyone was talking about online. Two days on the internet is an eternity. I'd rather do two *weeks* in the hole than two days on Twitter again—or whatever it's called now. It's impossible to keep track of that kind of stuff in here. One of the few perks of imprisonment.

It was too much for Gus to handle, I think, which is why he shut everything down, including the Manor. There was some relief, I guess, in believing that he wouldn't be coming back, that nobody else would be getting hurt or killed again. It didn't change the fact that my sister was dead, and that this great injustice had unfolded. I didn't only want the Manor to close. I wanted Gus behind bars. I wanted him to pay for what he had caused. It didn't matter to me that he hadn't physically been the one to kill Jessica. He was still the one responsible. As far as I was concerned, arresting Zach Chapman was only the beginning of what needed to be done. As it turned out, of course, it was the *only* course of action we'd see. Gus wasn't even *fined*. I couldn't believe it. None of us could. My sister was dead. I would never see or speak to her again, and Gus was free to continue operating as if nothing bad had happened at all.

HOWIE MCKINLEY

Truth be told, I might've been hopeful, after everything that had happened, that Gus would get his act straight and figure out something a little less…abnormal to do with his life. I was disappointed when he told me about his plans. We got into a big, heated argument about it. I asked him, "What are you gonna do when someone else dies on your property, son?" And…well, I guess he didn't really have an answer for that. He sort of grinned, like I was joking with him, like this was all some game. A few months later, he was gone.

JOHN BALTISBERGER

It did surprise me a little, when Gus reopened. You'd think, after everything that happened with the Henderson girl, he would have utilized better manners. He was a Texan, don't you forget, and in my book Texans ought to know better. I felt bad for the girl's family. The whole thing felt shameful. I was one of the first to know, too. He gave me a courtesy call ahead of time, told me what he was planning. I asked him, I said, "Gus, you sure that's such a wise idea?" And you know what he did? The fella laughed in my ear. He said, "Oh yeah, I'm positive." That might've been the last time we spoke, come to think about it. Because he only ever did do the one haunt after that—the one with the Henderson girl's brother, and he never bothered to warn us about it on the day of. We didn't find out that it was going on until after it ended.

TREVOR HENDERSON

I lost track of how many people sent me the video after it popped up on Gus's reactivated YouTube page. I must've been going over paperwork for college, or something like that. I never would go to college, of course. I suppose I could here in prison. They offer education, I'm told. There are courses available. But I guess I've never seen the point in it. It makes more sense for those with a future to look forward to. For someone in my position, though, it feels more masochistic than anything else. Why bother torturing myself?

My phone started blowing up. Everybody tagging and forwarding me the same link. I clicked it. The title was something like…MCKINLEY MANOR 2.0. I don't know. It was something goofy like that. But, basically, it was a trailer, I guess. Announcing the Manor's planned reopening in time for Halloween. What I remember most about the video, and what I'm sure everybody remembers, is the fact that he used Jessica's death as part of the promotion. That he advertised her murder as…as…as this *incentive*. Come to the scariest haunted house in the world! The haunted house so extreme you might not make it out alive!

It would have been bad enough if he's simply hinted at the death. But no. He fucking…well, you know what he did. It's why any of this happened. Why I'm in here. Why you're interviewing me.

He used her name.

He used her face.

A picture from her yearbook that had made the rounds in the initial news articles when everything first happened.

Are you tougher than Jessica Henderson? the video asked its audience. *Or are you just another scaredy-cat?*

Truth be told, it's impressive I *didn't* kill him.

CHRISTINE ADDAMS

I saw the video on Facebook. The one advertising he was reopening. I was so goddamn mad. After everything that had happened—and they were still allowing this nightmare to continue. A girl had died, but that didn't matter. None of it mattered. I should have burned it down. I really should have. Instead, I did nothing. I bitched about it a lot, but that was about it. What good was I? What good were any of us?

BETTY ROCKSTEADY

It was always Gus's plan to reopen. Not once had he intended to remain closed. The only reason the Manor went on hiatus at *all* was to allow a little time for things to calm down. He was pretty sure a lynch mob would have busted down his door if he tried operating as normal the following week. Plus, he said, going radio silent like he did, then reemerging a year later, it provided a certain theatrical element required for anyone in the haunt industry to successfully thrive. It added intrigue.

TREVOR HENDERSON

My parents were devastated when the video released. We thought about trying to sue, but it wasn't like we were loaded or anything. Lawyers are expensive. This wasn't a fight we could afford to start, nonetheless win. Instead they cried a lot. They stayed inside. They slept. We all did. What else could we do? Jessica had been dead for almost a year by then. We had spent that time trying to grieve but mostly controlling our rage for the psychopath who had caused her death. And now, suddenly, here he was again. Back in the public eye, fully prepared to use my sister's death as a selling point for the Manor.

I posted stuff online about him. I called him every name in the book. I told him he was a monster and a coward. I

The Last Haunt

figured he'd ignore it all. But Gus McKinley wasn't that type of person. The same people who sent me the trailer for his reopening started sending me more links leading me to Gus's public Facebook page. He'd uploaded these videos there which he'd recorded on his phone while driving. Basically recapping all the stuff I'd said about him. "It seems we got ourselves another hater!" I remember him shouting, then laughing his ass off like it was the funniest thing in the world, like I wasn't the brother of someone who had been killed in his haunted house.

He did, eventually, acknowledge who I was, though—and I'll tell you, I sure wish he hadn't. I'm paraphrasing here, but he basically told people I was Jessica's brother, and despite the law having carried swift justice with the arrest of Zach Chapman—"the person actually responsible for taking the incident too far"—I still wasn't satisfied. This was, of course, accurate, but the sarcastic way he said it, Jesus Christ, it felt like I was this big baby throwing a tantrum, you know what I mean?

And all the comments...man, you'd *think* at least one of them would have been on my side, right? Someone saying something like hey man, maybe you should give this guy a break, maybe what you're doing is totally insensitive and immoral? But no. Everybody was Team Gus. They were calling me a pussy. They were saying I was trying to...start drama...which, I mean. The drama had long started, wouldn't you say? And I certainly wasn't the one to start it.

And these accusations, these implications that I was somehow worse than Gus, they weren't limited to the comments. These people found me on every social. Facebook, Twitter, Instagram...and flooded my DMs. They were coming after me. For what? For being upset that my sister was dead, I guess. I don't know. Trying to understand the internet and what fuels a mob is an impossible, brain-aching science. The point is, they hated me. They were livid that I thought Gus was responsible for Jessica. They thought I was being cruel by even suggesting this. So, as revenge, they tried to drown me with threats. Threats against me, my parents, threats against…Jessica's corpse. So many of these motherfuckers promised to dig up her grave and violate her body. I couldn't believe it. The whole process was so overwhelming that it made me sick to my stomach. I couldn't breathe.

So I did the only thing I could think to do, and I deleted all of my accounts. I tried to disappear. Yet it didn't work. Somehow Gus recognized the potential in labeling me as this…villain. As this evil man trying to sabotage his business.

Looking back on it, I'm reminded of professional wrestling. Gus wanted me to play the heel. He knew his fans needed to hate *someone*, and if not me then who? How long before they turned their claws on Gus himself? I was a distraction, and Gus did not want to lose me. So he kept making videos. He claimed I was leading a hate group against the Manor, that I was still trying to shut it down. None of this was true. All I ever did was post some shit on my own personal accounts. I never started any anti-Gus groups. I never had that kind of ambition. I was in mourning. I was *grieving.*

Letters started showing up in our mailbox. Mean, ugly letters—somehow crueler than the ones I'd received online. I couldn't believe how heartless these people were being. I mean, they *knew* I was Jessica's brother. But, the thing I soon discovered is Jessica was also considered one of their enemies. Because of her, the Manor had almost gotten shut down. They thought the only reason Jessica died was because she hadn't properly trained and prepared her body. There was never any fault placed on Gus. To them, he was the victim in all this.

I don't know how I got the idea to do what I did. I guess I thought if I didn't do *something* then it would never end. And I figured the only way to shut him up would be to prove what most people who criticized the Manor already suspected but couldn't confirm:

The Last Haunt

That the prize money wasn't real, and the haunted house itself had never existed in the first place.

Making my audition video was a surreal experience. I was struck with the realization that my sister must've gone through the same process. She answered the same questions I answered. I never watched hers. I suppose at one point it must've been available in their Facebook group, or maybe the YouTube page—but by the time I had a reason to be invested in the Manor, that particular audition video had long been scrubbed.

And, honestly, I'm sort of relieved. I don't think I would have been able to watch her audition for what essentially became her own death, and I know for a fact I wouldn't have had to willpower *not* to watch it, either. I would have watched it every night as I cried myself to sleep. Although, to be fair, I still cried myself to sleep every night anyway, so maybe it wouldn't have mattered all that much in the grand scheme of things. [*Laughs.*] Jesus. What a fucked-up life this is for us all. You ever wonder why we bother sometimes?

The questions I had to address in my audition video felt standard. I had to explain who I was and why I wanted to do the haunt. I had to talk about my greatest fears. Stuff like that. I made it no secret that I was Jessica's brother. In fact it was what I led with. I said, "My name is Trevor Henderson and one year ago McKinley Manor murdered my sister Jessica Henderson on Halloween night." I told them that I was sick of the online abuse and I wanted his cult to leave me and my family alone once and for all. I suggested, to put an end to this drama, that he accept my audition. "I challenge you to a rematch, Gus," I said into my phone, spinning it exactly like how a wrestler might, really feeding into the entertainment soap opera charade of the whole thing.

I knew he wouldn't be able to resist that kind of…exaggerated showmanship. It's what he was all about, right? Above everything else, he was all about the *entertainment* factor, right? It didn't matter if someone died or not—as long as it was *entertaining*, right? *Right?*

[*Long pause.*]

Within one hour of submitting my audition, Gus posted the video on his public Facebook page. Not the *secret* group. His regular page, which had thousands and thousands of followers.

Let it never be said that Gus wasn't popular. The man had an audience, and they were all psychopaths and losers.

So he posts my video, and he says something like, "What do you say, folks? Do we get the crybaby a chance?" and, I kid you not, within ten minutes the comments were surpassing triple digits. Most were excited about the idea. Others simply chimed in to call me derogatory names. Way too many of them cracked jokes about my sister. A smarter person would have never read the comments. I guess you could also say a smarter person would have never engaged with Gus in the first place. But that doesn't really matter now, does it?

I was granted access to the infamous Facebook group. I think there were about thirty thousand members in it already, but the thing about that number is it never seemed to *increase* all that much. If anything the number shrunk on a daily basis. I'm not really sure what the deal was there. People sick of Gus's crap? People getting banned for violating the group's bizarre rules? There was a lot of stuff in the guidelines about not associating with hate groups, but not the hate groups you might be thinking—specifically, hate against Gus and the Manor. Did those types of groups exist, though? There were a few I found, but all of them were *also* hidden behind private groups, and I was never granted access when I requested to join them, so I have no idea what was actually going on there. Did they think, because of my name, and who that name is associated with, I might've been a fake account designed to spy on them?

It was decided that I would do McKinley Manor on

Halloween, one month from when I auditioned, and one year from Jessica's haunt. Like every haunt, it would be livestreamed in the group for everybody to watch along at home. But, before I could attend the Manor, I would first have to complete a series of challenges from remote locations, which would also be streamed live for Gus and his fanboys.

I'd heard about these challenges while doing research prior to my audition. They were nothing more than juvenile fraternity hazings. Like recording myself doing funny dances in the grocery store, or eating extraordinarily strong hot sauces. One of the challenges involved tying a water bottle to my ceiling fan, then blindfolding myself and trying not to get smacked in the face as the fan spun the bottle around in circles. Under any other circumstances I would have found the whole thing hilariously stupid. Here was this so-called "extreme haunted house" wasting everybody's time by forcing me to participate in silly TikTok stunts. If I hadn't known better, I would have assumed these hazings were only introduced to fuck with me specifically, as punishment for "disparaging" the Manor. However, now that I had access to the Facebook group, I could easily go back and watch previous livestreams nobody had bothered to delete, and I was able to confirm these hazings were nothing new, and were in fact as pedestrian as the ones I was being forced to partake in. It was lame, and demeaning, but I kept telling myself it would be worth it, that I couldn't give up, that I had to go through with it all and prove Gus was ultimately full of shit. I had no intention of not completing the Manor. I didn't care if it killed *me*, too. I was going to make it to the end. I was determined. And then, when Gus couldn't pay me the prize money, everybody watching the livestream would finally understand it had all been a lie.

I never wanted my parents to find out about my recent online interactions with Gus and our plans to meet up. It was my hope that, somehow, the news would never reach them, that I would manage to keep them shielded from everything happening. I knew they would go crazy if they learned I was going to do the haunt, and they would be absolutely justified with this reaction. They had lost their daughter the exact same way, after all. Why on earth would their son decide to do it, too? I couldn't conceive of a logical explanation for them, so I hoped like hell I never had to. Unfortunately, someone snitched. I don't know who, and I suppose it doesn't matter now. But yeah. They found out, and they were pissed. Well, first they were angry, but once they realized this wasn't a joke and that I was serious, the anger transformed into more of a desperate panic. They tried pleading with me, offering all sorts of things if only I changed my mind. My dad offered to buy me a car—which, if you know my dad, is such an out-of-character gesture that it knocked me on my ass when he first brought it up. I was determined. I told them I didn't expect them to understand, but this was the right thing to do. For Jessica, I told them. I was doing this for Jessica.

Anyway. It's no surprise to me that they refuse to speak to you for this little book you're compiling. Take a guess how many times they've bothered visiting me in here. [*Laughs.*] Can't say I blame them any, though. The bitch of the whole thing being was they were right. I *shouldn't* have gone to the Manor. I should have stayed far away and lived a real life. *That's* what Jessica would have wanted.

Not…*this*.

I didn't have a car, and my parents obviously weren't willing to let me borrow theirs, so I wasn't left with a whole lot of choices. I didn't have a job either, so it wasn't like I had the funds to Uber around or anything. That stuff adds up after so long, you know? But I *could* afford a bus ticket, so that's what I did. From San Antonio it was about a four-hour drive to Pork Basket. On a bus, that became a six-hour ride. I left early Halloween morning, before the sun had risen, and we

The Last Haunt

pulled up sometime that afternoon. Unsurprisingly, I was the only passenger who got off at my stop.

I wasn't scheduled to meet up with Gus until around three, but since I was planning on traveling around town by foot, that didn't really leave me a lot of time to loiter. Especially since I still needed to acquire a fifty-pound bag of dog food, which would act as my entrance fee for the Manor. Fortunately I'd already purchased the animal onesie everybody's required to wear during the haunt—a pink rabbit costume, kinda similar to the one that kid wore in *A Christmas Story*. And, before you think I was crazy enough to have worn it on the bus into town, I'd stuffed the onesie in my backpack. I wasn't gonna put it on any earlier than absolutely necessary.

As for the dog food, I was instructed to purchase it at a local pet shop, but after consulting the map app on my phone, I realized how much shorter of a walk it'd be if I simply snagged a bag at a Walmart near Gus's house. I'd already known about the Walmart because in Gus's instructions he had made a weird point to forbid me from entering that specific location. With everything else going on, it barely registered how silly of a rule this was until I was actually *in* Pork Basket and looking at the map app. There was no way I was going to walk to the other side of town, buy a fifty-pound bag of dog food, then walk all the way back while carrying it due to some arbitrary rule.

So I went to the Walmart, and that was when I saw Gus's framed picture on the EMPLOYEES OF THE MONTH shrine next to the public bathrooms, and suddenly a lot of things made sense. He didn't want me shopping at Walmart because he didn't want me to find out that's where he worked. See, this was a part of his life that *wasn't* public knowledge, which was rare for someone like Gus, who tended to post and stream every stupid microscopic thought that infiltrated his skull.

Why wouldn't he want anybody finding out about this, though? A few reasons, I suppose. One, he was embarrassed.

And two, he feared how his so-called "haters" might use it to their advantage. He probably thought a) they'd make fun of him online about it and b) they'd harass him there until he was fired. I imagine enough people calling anybody's place of employment day and night would be enough to get most people terminated, but someone like Gus who already had plenty of awful—though justified—press on the internet for anybody to find? There's no way he would have made it.

I'll admit that I immediately started racking my brains for ways to use this information for sabotage. This was the man responsible for my sister's death. He deserved to burn. First I snuck around the store trying to make sure he wasn't currently working a shift. If I bumped into him there, I was sure he would have cancelled our plans. Probably would have made up something like I wasn't truly dedicated to the haunt, or whatever bullshit he used to tell his fans. But I didn't see him.

So I got a shopping cart, I threw the cheapest fifty-pound bag of dog food in the basket, and walked around until I spotted an employee. There was this one lady counting milk cartons in the dairy section. I asked her about Gus, and the look on her face was priceless. I was not expecting her—or, as it turned out, *everybody* who worked there—to already know about the Manor. I guess I assumed he would have hidden that from them like he'd hidden the Walmart job from everybody else, but that wasn't the case at all.

From the way I heard it, the Manor was all he ever talked about, and his coworkers thought he was a nutcase. Nobody there actually liked him. They barely tolerated him. The milk lady noticed the dog food in my cart and correctly guessed why I was there. She told me it was a damn good thing Gus wasn't on the schedule today, because the last time one of his "contestants" showed up here while he was working, the shit hit the fan. She told me Gus blew up on the guy. Got in his face and was yelling, calling him all sorts of names that questioned his intelligence. It was nasty, she said. I asked her how Gus managed not to get fired after something like that, and all she did was shrug and suggest that since he was a retired veteran, termination wasn't the simplest of processes. In other words, he wasn't going anywhere any time soon.

Little did she know how wrong she was, though—right? [*Laughs.*]

ZACH CHAPMAN

I was incarcerated when the massacre went down. This was still early in my sentence. The previous year, after everything with Jessica, how it blew up on the news and internet, the trial had not been long, and the jury did not need an extensive deliberation before coming up with a verdict. I wouldn't learn about what happened to Gus and the others for a couple days. News doesn't travel fast in prison. Information comes through, but it can take time. To be perfectly honest? I wish I'd never found out. I wish, somehow, this particular bit of news had remained hidden from me forever.

TREVOR HENDERSON

Like every participant, I was supposed to meet him and his crew at a nearby park instead of the actual Manor. This proved to be a slightly more difficult walk than I anticipated, largely due to the fact that there wasn't a sidewalk or noticeable trail leading from Walmart to the park, so I was forced to dodge traffic on the edge of a busy farm-to-market road—all while carrying a fifty-pound bag of dog food. By the time I made it to the park, Gus and his guys were already there waiting on me. I was ten minutes late and already exhausted, drenched in sweat. Texas Octobers can sometimes be jacket-weather and sometimes so hot you shouldn't bother leaving the house until the sun goes down. This particular October happened to be the latter. So already I was thinking oh man, have I doomed myself before we've started?

Plus, like I said, I was a little late, and Gus made sure to throw a big hissy fit about that the moment I was within hearing range. Kept acting like he was debating calling everything off, that if I couldn't treat our agreed-upon time seriously then how could he trust me to take the rest of the haunt seriously. But I knew he was bluffing. He wasn't going to cancel something like this over a lousy ten minutes. Not with all the buzz it had already built in the Facebook group. His fans had been dying to watch this stream for a month now. He wasn't going to deny them what they wanted, and what they wanted was to see me get tortured.

The first thing Gus made me do was change into my animal onesie—the pink rabbit costume I mentioned was in my backpack. He wouldn't start recording until it was fully on my body. He said it shattered the "world building" if people saw me in regular clothes. Something I noticed right away was how different he sounded in real life compared to the life streams, or the random diary-style videos he'd post on his personal account. There was no sense of showmanship here. He sounded like a regular guy. A little tired, a little antsy, but there was no trace of the evil motherfucker I'd grown to loathe over the last year.

He didn't come out until the streaming started. Once the phone was recording, he turned into the person I'd been expecting to find here. Him and the rest of his goddamn crew.

There were three of them total. All wearing those stupid pillowcases over their heads. Gus, of course, then two others. I didn't know their names then, but you bet I'd learn them later on, once I was charged with each of their murders.

Gus McKinley.

Trey Hudson.

The Last Haunt

Rick LaRocca.

Trey and Rick looked to be around my age. Just like the other one—Zachary Chapman—the kid who served time for my sister's death. Far less time than what the state sentenced me with. You know, they say the longer you're in here, the less spiteful you become, but I think that couldn't be further from the truth. Every night I go to sleep in a cell, my hatred for Texas only seems to intensify. He literally drowned my sister, and he's out now walking free as a bird. I wonder if he considers himself grateful. I wonder if he realizes how lucky he is that he wasn't at the Manor with everybody else that Halloween night. Because if he had been, he sure as shit wouldn't be alive today. And I don't mean that in a threatening way to imply that *I* would have killed him. I'm just saying...*something* would have killed him. *Something* would have ensured he never made it to November. Something like...

...well, okay. We might be getting ahead of ourselves here.

I'll get to that soon.

To what killed everybody.

Although...if you've already read the court transcripts, you can already take a safe guess as to what I'm going to tell you.

But first—the contract.

I don't know how many pages it actually was. I didn't count. He made sure to go over every single clause. I've read online that up until Jessica's death, people thought the contract was this bullshit scare tactic, and I can understand why. He spent like two hours seated across from me, making sure I heard every possible thing that might happen—including, yes, getting crushed to death by a wall of spikes. [*Laughs.*] Most of the stuff in it wasn't real, I think that was clear to everybody with half a brain. If I hadn't already done my research on what to expect, I *can* see how the contract might have spooked me a little. It did a good job of making the imagination go wild. That, plus it's super long, and tedious, and time-consuming, so any participant going over everything is bound to get drained from that alone. I imagine that's its true purpose. To tire you out early on.

But, with that said, this time the contract worked to Gus's disadvantage, because by the time I made it to the park I was already exhausted from the long walk. If anything, I was *relieved* to sit on a bench going over a bunch of paperwork. It allowed time for me to catch a second wind before the real physical activities kicked off. If he had forced me to immediately get into the grit of it all, I would have most likely passed out within the first ten minutes.

Instead, I got my rest. I was able to revitalize myself while he talked shit. Saying stuff like I couldn't handle the haunt, that I better give up now before it's too late, that they didn't want what happened to my sister to happen to me, too. I tried my best to ignore it all. They wanted a reaction and I wasn't about to give it to them. I had already done my part in his little soap opera. Now that I was here, my only concern was not giving up and making it where nobody else had ever reached. I wasn't going to leave until he was forced to admit that the prize money didn't exist, and my sister had died trying to win something she could have never realistically won.

I trained ahead of time, yeah. I didn't want to show up and immediately tap out. That would have accomplished nothing except stroke Gus's ego. But, like, don't get me wrong. I was in okay shape, sure, but I wasn't an *athlete* or anything like that. I spent most of my time watching YouTube and eating potato chips. The months following Jessica's death, the only time I left the house was to take the trash out or mow the lawn, and that was only after my parents got on my ass when the HOA threatened to fine us for the grass getting too wild.

The Last Haunt

But in the month leading up to Halloween—all throughout October—I was hit with a new motivation I had never experienced before. I guess you can call it revenge. If a better word exists, it's not one that's in my vocabulary.

I ran every morning. I counted calories. I lifted my dad's weights in our garage.

I did other things, too. Things that I couldn't explain to anyone without them potentially freaking out on me.

I started taking these long baths. In the beginning, I'd dunk my head under and see how long I could hold my breath.

Once that got boring, I mixed it up a little.

I got a washcloth and put it over my face, then turned the shower hose to maximum pressure, and I let that baby rip.

Let me tell you this: it is *not* easy to waterboard yourself.

I don't know if that's a no-shit statement or not. But I think I expected it to be simpler than what it ended up being. For one thing, I couldn't believe how terrifying it was. The first time I did it, I started sobbing and I didn't stop until I fell asleep later that night. All I could think about was what Jessica must have gone through, what her final thoughts must've been. When water's blasting you directly in your face like that, and you can't breathe, you stop thinking logically. There is no such thing as a coherent train of thought. All of your senses spiral into full panic. It is impossible to train yourself to be okay with this. Nobody can survive being drowned. I don't care how tough you are.

But they *can* learn to tolerate it longer than others. And that is what I did. I practiced and practiced and went longer and longer. The fear never went away. The panic remained. But I forced myself to control it—if only briefly. You ever see that trivia online about people in the CIA tapping out after less than half a minute? Think about that, now think about what Gus was doing, and you tell me how anybody was realistically meant to complete the Manor.

Once we were finished with the contract, we got right into it.

Nobody else was at the park—just me, Gus, and the other two guys.

You know those electronic collars you put on dogs to stop them from barking? They strapped one of those to my bare calf, under the animal onesie, which they could control with a remote controller. Throughout the haunt they'd zap me whenever I wasn't doing something fast enough, or whenever they were feeling especially bored, I guess. They also had me wear these bizarre glasses that made everything appear upside down. Something you'd buy at a magic store. I wanted to take them off the moment they were on, but they told me if I couldn't handle the glasses then I sure as hell couldn't handle the rest of the haunt.

Now, if you've watched any of the livestream videos, you'll know that these haunts were less about being scary and more about being exhausting. Gus liked to use words like "terrifying" when a more accurate description would have been "tiring." The first thing he had me do was jumping jacks, followed by pushups, then sit ups, then more jumping jacks. We did that for a half hour while Gus filmed me, and Rick and Trey tried taunting me with insults about my masculinity. It still makes me laugh knowing how many people were watching along at home. Maybe "laugh" isn't the right word. This bullshit killed my sister. But still. It was so *stupid*. It was so *silly*. How was any of this entertaining? What was the *point*?

After the basic exercises, we upgraded to crab walking. You know—like in *The Exorcist*? But this wasn't normal crab walking. No, buddy. This was *extreme* crab walking. [*Laughs.*] Meaning, they made me hold the fifty-pound bag of dog food in my lap the whole time. It wasn't easy, but that didn't make it any less ridiculous. We did that off and on for about another half hour, then they led me toward a drainage ditch, tired my

The Last Haunt

arms and legs together, and had me crawl back and forth for a while with the bag of dog food on my back until I inevitably collapsed from exhaustion.

Once it was clear that I could no longer move, Trey and Rick got down into the ditch and flipped me over so I was sprawled out on my back. The bag of dog food was cast off somewhere to the side. I was still tied up pretty good, both my wrists and my ankles. So I couldn't really fight back if I wanted to, which I didn't. I was going to let them do whatever it was they wanted to do. I wasn't going to give up. And what they wanted to do was spray my face with paint. The paint was in what looked like mustard and ketchup bottles. Solid red, solid yellow. But it was paint. Green and blue paint. Gus stood off to the side while Trey squeezed the bottles. I remember Gus groaning and breathing real heavy, and saying stuff like, "Paint his face, paint the coward's face."

After the face painting, they took clothespins to my lips and cheeks and spread my mouth open so it looked like I had this permanent, psychotic grin.

It was bizarre, man.

They decided we had been at the park long enough, and it was time to go to the Manor. They took off the clothespins and upside-down glasses and blindfolded me proper, then led me to their van and threw me in the back. They put these headphones over my ears, too, and I had to listen to the lamest recording imaginable. I don't remember the audio verbatim. It was something Gus had recorded. Something really cheesy but it was obvious *he* thought it would scare people. I know, in the recording, he kept calling me a sheep. Lots of, "Welcome, sheep," and, "You are mine now, sheep," stuff. He'd repeat all these phrases over and over like he was trying to hypnotize me. I don't know. It was difficult to concentrate. I wasn't fastened, either. Part of the so-called "thrill" was watching me get banged up as Gus drove around like an asshole. I would remain blindfolded for the rest of the haunt, by the way. They wanted me to imagine something far scarier than the reality of the Manor.

The van stopped. I didn't know if we were at the Manor yet or what—it would turn out, yes, we were parked in the driveway. I would hope by now you've made it clear in your book that the Manor was also just…Gus's house. This was where he lived. There was no grand haunted house or anything. He made people do exhausting exercises at the park, then he brought them back to his house out in the suburbs.

Before we got out of the van, Gus and his guys all got into the back and proceeded to beat the shit out of me. They punched and kicked and spit on me. There was nothing creative about it. You should've seen the bruises on my ribs the next day. They would stomp on my stomach and then ask if I gave up yet. When I said no, they'd punch me in the kidneys and ask, "How about now?" Once it became clear that I wasn't going to surrender, they threw me out of the van and dragged me to the back yard, where neighbors couldn't see over Gus's perimeter fencing. I'm sure they could still hear us, though—and, sadly, I'm sure they were used to it by then.

ZACH CHAPMAN

You know, after I got locked up, Gus told me I could call him anytime I needed to talk to someone, and he'd always pick up. I thought he might've been bullshitting, you know? But he was a man of his word. He always answered. Well, until the day he didn't.

TREVOR HENDERSON

I thought I had prepared ahead of time by studying previous streams and researching the Manor's layout via Google Maps, but once I was in the thick of it all, I could barely concentrate on which way I was walking. I couldn't think straight. If you'd asked me my name at the time, I'm not sure I would have been able to tell you. All I knew was I was in a massive amount of pain, I was hot, I was exhausted, and I wanted to go home—which is how everybody was meant to feel by the time they reached this point—*if* they reached this point. I saw plenty of videos where others tapped out back at the park. And you know what? After experiencing the process firsthand, I don't blame them one bit. It still amazes me that I made it through what I did.

When we reached the back of the Manor, someone guided my shoulder and made me spin around in circles until I could no longer stand. It wouldn't have taken much to make me fall down, anyway, considering they still had my ankles tied together. They stood far away from me and shouted my name, demanding I follow the sounds of their voices, but of course I kept tripping and getting myself all banged up on random shit they had boobytrapping the back yard. You know how many goddamn gnomes were planted in that yard? It was like walking through a landmine field. The whole point of any of this was to continually make me disoriented and tired. They might've advertised themselves as a haunted house attraction, but it was clear they weren't that interested in the "spooky" aspect of it all. They didn't want to scare you. They wanted to defeat you. Even if that meant killing you.

Speaking of—it was around then they started in with the waterboarding. What they did was they had me get into this large barrel, then they chained my arms against my chest and forced my head to lean back. I had been waiting for this moment. Training for it. Yet, when that hose first blasted into my face, the only thing I could think was, *I am going to die.* You could waterboard anybody and it'll always be their natural instinct, to believe that death is inevitable. When you waterboard someone, you are cutting off their oxygen supply. They literally can't breathe. If you fuck around and do it too long, you will kill someone. You will fucking murder them. And then, a year after you've murdered them, the victim's idiotic brother will show up to the same place and volunteer for you to do the exact same thing to them, too. Why? Like I already said. They're a fucking idiot. But that's what will happen, because that's what happened, right? I let them waterboard me for their ridiculous, sadistic livestream show. I thought I was going to die. I couldn't stand it, but I refused to give up. I would have preferred they kill me just as they killed my sister before I surrendered. And maybe Gus realized this, too, because after a while he finally called it, said I'd had enough, and it was time to do Scorpion Scramble—something my sister had never survived long enough to participate in.

According to Gus, once you won Scorpion Scramble, you would graduate from the pre-haunt training part of the tour and be granted access to the real haunted house. Before I showed up to the Manor, I obsessed over every single recorded stream available on both YouTube and in their Facebook group. I found zero evidence that anybody had ever defeated Scorpion Scramble. And that's because, as we all know now, there was *nothing* after it. There was no haunted house. There was the torture boot camp bullshit and that was it.

Gus made sure that nobody could realistically win Scorpion Scramble. It was basically this shitty, DIY metal maze him and his crew had built in the back yard. Just tall and wide enough for a person to crawl through. You were supposed to make it through the maze while blindfolded—plus, your wrists and ankles were still tied together, so it was

The Last Haunt

less of a crawling motion and more of a…wiggling, I guess. At the end of the maze, once you unlocked the exit contraption with your mouth—a bucket of deadly scorpions was meant to drop all over you. After you felt the scorpions on your body, you were supposed to "scramble" them loose and stand up, scorpion-free. Oh, and the whole time you're maneuvering through the maze? Someone's standing on top of the metal grating system blasting your face with the hose. So, instead of waterboarding increments like what they were doing back at the barrel, it now became one continuous session.

Maybe it's redundant to mention at this point, but the bucket of "deadly scorpions" didn't exist. Nobody was going to make it that far. Or so Gus assumed. There had been a few streams in the past where it looked like they might get to the exit. Usually, when that would happen, Gus would make the judgement call to end the haunt, citing that he was concerned about the person's health and didn't want them to die of hypothermia or something. But really it was just an excuse to end things before he got called out on his bullshit.

So why, then, did Gus not pull the same stunt with me?

Well, I've had a lot of time to think about this question. That's what prison is for, right? Going over the *whys* of your past. And I think—nah, I *know* why Gus didn't pull me out of Scorpion Scramble when it became clear that I wasn't going to tap out. Do you know what kind of publicity the Manor received after my sister died? For an extreme "haunted house," any press is good press—especially negative press, because it feeds into the advertisement, right? There's no need to go through the hard work of convincing everybody you're the most extreme haunt in the world if the nightly news is doing it for you. So, I think Gus was trying to do it again. I think he was hoping I died in that maze, drowned due to my own stubbornness to avenge my sister. Could you imagine the headlines? Extreme Haunt Slays Second Henderson

Offspring. He'd go down in the history books. Plus, he'd already gotten away with it once. After all, *he* wasn't the one handling the hose. Look at what happened with the Chapman kid. He took the fall and Gus faced zero consequences. In fact, he wasn't even prevented from reopening the following year. He could get away with anything at that point. He was untouchable. So he thought, why not let this idiot kid die on his livestream? That was what got people's attention: real death.

That's what I figure he was thinking, anyway. Speculation, though, that's about all we can do at this point. It's not like you can go ask him about it after you're done talking to me. [*Laughs.*]

The escape door at the end of the maze supposedly had a lock on it, but it was designed in such a way nobody could realistically open it while blindfolded and tied up. But I was determined, and I managed to break the goddamn thing off its tiny hinges with my head and crawl out. I waited for the scorpions to fall, and they never did.

I started laughing. Like, really hard, and crazy. I think I might've spooked them all. And imagining *them* getting spooked only made me laugh harder.

"Where's the scorpions at, Gus?" I shouted, and he stammered out some embarrassing excuse about it being my lucky day, that he was in-between scorpions at the moment. He said he had to routinely swap buckets with fresh ones, and the night of my haunt just so happened to fall on the one night of the month he wasn't stocked with new inventory. I wondered if anybody else watching at home found this explanation as funny as I did, because I sure as hell thought it was the funniest possible thing he could have told me. By then, the blindfold had slid halfway down my face. Maybe from all the water pressure blasting against me. It was dark now, which I'd already gathered earlier from the lack of light shining through the blindfold. But now I could *really* see, and there was Gus with his silly pillowcase over his face. I could see his eyes, though, and those eyes told a story. There was rage in those eyes. There was violence.

"Okay, Gus," I said, "I'm ready for this haunted house."

Immediately he was on the defense. "You think there's no haunted house, don't you?" he said. And I said, "Are you gonna take me there or not? Everybody's waiting." It was clear he was feeling the pressure. He got fidgety behind the camera. Started looking around like he was trying to make a decision about something. "Okay," he said, "I'll take you to the haunted house. But I might as well warn you one last time: you really don't want to do this."

I shook my head and told him I absolutely wanted to do this.

He gestured for his two goons to help me up to my feet. "C'mon," he told them, "let's take Mr. Henderson here to the haunted house." And they both hesitated, staring at him, before Gus shouted, "I said pick him up, *goddammit*!" Someone more knowledgeable about McKinley Manor might be able to correct me here, but I am almost positive that is the only time he'd ever used profanity during one of his livestreams. That was how I knew I had him. He said goddammit, which meant he was fucked.

But, as you and everybody else knows, Gus was quick on his feet. He already had a plan in motion. Halfway across the yard toward his house, he told everybody to stop. His tone had changed. "Oh, gosh," he said, calm and collected, "fellas, I hate to be the bearer of bad news, but it looks like my camera battery is seconds away from dying."

I stared at him like he was insane, which he was. "Don't you have a backup?" I asked him, and he said, "This *is* my backup." Then he told me that maybe if I hadn't taken so long completing boot camp, that if I'd spent a little more time doing the tasks and a little less time whining, maybe we could have done the haunted house. But I was too slow, and now we had to call it a night. The last thing he said before shutting off the camera was, "Good night, everybody, thank you for joining us. I hope you've had just as much fun as we've had."

And that was it. That was the end of the stream. The last stream he'd ever record.

JOHN BALTISBERGER

We got a call late that night from a neighbor. She said there was something going on over at Gus's house. People were screaming—not one person but many. "Something is different," the neighbor told us. "This isn't like how it used to be." I listened to my instincts, and I took a drive out to Gus's. As it turned out, I was way too late. What was done was done. You haven't asked, but I'll tell you. Seeing what I saw in that back yard…it took all but two seconds for me to decide on an early retirement from the force. When I signed up to be a cop all those years ago, I never wanted to see…what it was I saw. You don't become a cop for the opportunity to stumble upon the inside of another human being. At least I sure as hell didn't. Looking around at the carnage at Gus's house, I didn't know what had happened, but I did know I didn't want anything to do with it. I was done.

CHRISTINE ADDAMS

I was the one who called the cops—big surprise, right? Almost like we've come full circle here, huh? Almost like I warned them enough not to let this fucking horror show remain open. However, if I had known who the real victim was this time, I would've never bothered picking up my phone. The cocksucker more than deserved it, if you ask me.

ZACH CHAPMAN

That night everything happened—don't forget, that shit was Halloween night. One-year anniversary of what I'd done to Jessica Henderson. It's fucking spooky, you know? Especially once you hear what her brother had to say about it all. Most folks thought he was nuts, right? Just an absolute goddamn lunatic who snapped and went berserk. And, you know, maybe that's true, right? Maybe that *is* what happened. But I don't know, man. Sometimes I don't know what to believe.

HOWIE MCKINLEY

Sir, I'm sorry, but I don't think I can continue this interview.

TREVOR HENDERSON

Look, I'm not an idiot, okay? I know I'm never going to see the sun rise again in my life. Yes, there is the possibility of parole a few years down the road, but I think we both know the likelihood of something like that happening. If they give me parole, then they're admitting to the impossible, and that's something they will never do. This prison is my home now, and I will never know anywhere different.

So what I'm going to say next, I am saying it because it is the truth, not because I believe it will help me walk out of here a free man. I know it won't. But I also can't live with myself accepting a fictionalized version of the events. I know what I witnessed. I am, in fact, the only living witness from that night able to testify. You won't believe me, because to believe me is to open a door in your brain no human can afford to unlock. But that's okay. In the beginning, when I was first imprisoned,

I found myself full of anger that everybody rejected what I had to say. But I've come to accept it. I've put myself in their shoes, and I wouldn't want to believe something like this, either.

But, unfortunately, I don't have the luxury of being an outsider.

I was there, and this is what happened:

In that first minute, once Gus turned off the camera, I stood there in total astonishment. "Did you really just do that?" I said, and once again his whole showmanship persona had vanished. Erased. He removed the pillowcase from his face. "Do what?" he said. "I told you. The camera died." Then, to his goons, he said, "Get him untied. This tour is officially over."

As Trey and Rick released me from the restraints, I couldn't take my eyes off Gus. I told him, "So, I guess that means you owe me fifty thousand dollars," and he laughed a little like how I'd laughed during Scorpion Scramble. "What are you talking about?" he said, like he didn't already know. I told him I hadn't given up. I hadn't quit. *He* was the one who quit. This meant I won the prize money. According to the rules, all I had to do was make it through the haunt without quitting, and I'd win the money. That was when Trey started piping in. "You ain't make it through the haunt, dipshit," he said, "you ain't even start it yet."

"Well," I said, "then how about you take me to it? I'm ready to continue."

Trey raised his fist like he was going to strike me, then stopped. "He already told you," he said, "the goddamn battery's dead. We can't film!"

"So what?" I said. "Why do you need to film? I'm here. You're all here. Let's continue."

"Quit acting tough, little boy," Gus said, still laughing, "or I'll have to inform folks how you broke one of my most essential rules right from the get-go. You're lucky I let that slide, by the way."

The Last Haunt

"*What* rule?" I said, genuinely confused.

"You think I didn't recognize where you bought that dog food?" he said, then told Trey and Rick to pack everything up, it was time to call it a night. I said some more stuff, but they ignored me. Gus instructed them to drive me back to the park in the van. It wasn't like Gus had anywhere to go. He was already home. All he had to do was go inside. I could tell, too, that he desperately wanted to do exactly that. He was tired. It'd been a long day for him.

But I was determined. I was *pissed*. I'd made it through their bullshit haunt—or *boot camp,* or whatever they wanted to call it—and I wasn't leaving until they either paid me the fifty-thousand dollars or admitted the prize money never existed in the first place. Of course, looking back now, I don't know what I hoped to accomplish with the livestream being turned off. It wouldn't have mattered if he *had* admitted the truth, nobody would have believed me. It makes you wonder why he didn't go ahead and say it, right? Just to get me to leave. Maybe because of the two guys working for him. Did they buy into all of Gus's bullshit? They must have, right? Otherwise, what were they doing there?

"I'm not leaving," I told them again, and started digging into my backpack. Someone must've brought it out of the van with us when we got to the Manor. I don't know why or who. Gus asked what I was doing, and I replied with the truth: I was searching for my cellphone. "If you guys need an extra camera," I said, "I'm pretty sure my battery is full."

Gus, man, he turned cold as stone after that. He said, "Don't even think about it, boy. I told you the tour was over, and my word is final."

"But I didn't give up," I said, at long last locating my phone and pulling it out.

That was when something hit me in the back of the head, and my body dropped.

When I rolled over, I saw Trey standing above me

holding a zombie garden gnome. The ceramic was cracked in half, and pieces of it were crumbling out of his hand. I remember thinking, *My skull is the reason for this*, before time skipped a beat, and everything got a little hazy.

A few minutes passed.

Things started returning to focus. I was still flat on my back, head throbbing like it was about to explode, or maybe already *had* exploded. Nobody had moved me or touched me since the initial strike, as far as I could tell.

It had started to rain.

Nothing too hard. At least not yet. A light trickle. But it was cold and wet enough to shock me from unconsciousness.

Gus was arguing with Trey about something. I couldn't make out what they were saying. But Gus was fucking *pissed*, that much was clear.

I opened my eyes and saw Rick kneeling next to me.

"Hey, guys," he said, shouting at the others, "he's alive! He's alive!"

I think I may have said something then, but I don't remember what it was, or if it made any sense. I tried to sit up, but everything was dizzy, disorienting. I fell back down.

Gus and Trey walked over to us. Nobody had the pillowcases over their heads anymore. You'd assume Gus wouldn't have given a shit if I lived or died. After all, look at how he'd benefited from my sister. He should've been *rooting* for my death. Except, of course, the key difference here is Jessica had died *on camera*. True, the recording of Jessica's death was supposedly erased the moment after it finished, but there had still been witnesses watching it stream live. With me, it was a different story. When my stream ended, I was still breathing. If I died *after* the fact, where was the proof that Gus hadn't been directly responsible? That, and…it's sickening to say, but putting myself in his point-of-view…where was the *glory* of capturing another death on camera? It would have been such a missed opportunity for him.

The Last Haunt

So, yeah. [*Laughs.*] He was not a happy camper.

Standing above me, he asked if I was okay, and I mumbled something that he must have understood, because he nodded and said in this obviously forced jokey tone, "I thought we were the ones supposed to scare *you*, not the other way around!"

Behind him, Trey said, "What are we going to do?" and Gus snapped at him and screamed, "*Didn't I tell you to shut the fuck up?*"

I don't know if they noticed, but the rain was falling heavier now. I had to turn my head to the side to avoid choking on it. I think Gus and Trey were too busy bickering again. Trey wasn't backing down from Gus's latest burst of hostility. He started saying stuff like, "You can't talk to me like that," and, "I thought you wanted me to hit him." Gus was in full denial mode, claiming he didn't know what Trey was talking about, accusing Trey of being on drugs. Meanwhile Rick stood off to the side with his hands in his pockets. You could tell he was feeling awkward and uncomfortable about the whole thing and didn't know what to do about it. Debating whether or not he should've turned around and bailed—and it's a shame he didn't. Maybe he'd still be alive today.

The rain was getting intense. I couldn't keep lying there like that. It took some doing, but I was able to sit up without collapsing. Everything was still a little dizzy, but more manageable now. I wasn't at a point where I could stand yet, but I was content to sit in the rain. Something about it felt calming—reassuring. Like it was here to comfort me.

Then Rick said, "Hey, who's that?"

Gus and Trey stopped arguing. We all looked at Rick, then followed the direction Rick was pointing:

Across the yard, at the barrel where they'd waterboarded me.

It had overflowed from the rainwater, but that wasn't

what had attracted Rick's attention—and it wasn't what captured ours.

[*Hesitates.*]

Okay, this is the part where I start talking about the stuff I warned you about. The stuff nobody believes. The whole reason, I suppose, that you're here talking to me today.

Someone was in the barrel.

All we could see were their hands and arms as they pulled themself up. Then—a face emerged from the rim. A woman's face. But she wasn't gasping like someone who might've been submerged by water. She was calm. She was *fine*, honestly.

It wasn't until she started crawling out of the barrel that we realized she didn't seem to have any skin.

Whatever she was made of, it was translucent. Like *water*. Not completely clear, though. She was *murky*. Dirty, almost.

I thought all the heavy rain pouring down was screwing with my sight. A trick of the eyes. But I know what I saw, and judging by the way everybody else there reacted, our perceptions weren't too dissimilar.

Someone—I think Gus—shouted, "Holy mother of god!"

I don't know if they ever realized who it was—who had climbed out of the barrel. I recognized her within seconds. It would have been weird if I hadn't. Every little brother ought to know the sight of his own sister, wouldn't you say?

But it wasn't only her appearance. It was her overall *presence*. Remember what I was saying about the rain feeling comforting? I wasn't being hyperbolic. That was my sister arriving.

That was her coming to save me.

We were mesmerized. What would you do if you saw a woman made of water coming toward you? Logic says you'd run, right? Well, nothing about that night was logical. It's easy to think about what you *should* have done about something after it's too late. Everybody can do that. But what they *can't*

The Last Haunt

do is know how they *will* react when it's their turn to face the supernatural. Because that's what this was, of course. The supernatural. Yes, it was Jessica, it was *my sister*, but I'm not crazy. I know she's dead. Yet there she was — somehow *back*. And she consisted entirely of the element responsible for her own demise.

Somewhere behind me, Rick said, "I think she needs help," and approached her.

Gus and Trey stayed back on the other side of the yard. Trey said something like, "I wouldn't touch that bitch if I were you. She looks crazy."

Either Rick didn't hear him, or he wasn't listening, because he continued toward my sister. She was standing next to the barrel, not really moving, just staring at us. No expression. No emotion.

He stopped in front of her. He said something. I don't know what. The rain was coming down too hard to hear anything. Then Rick fell to his knees, still gazing up at her. He didn't seem to be in pain. It was more like it was an…act of *honor*, if that makes any sense? Like it would have been rude if he *hadn't* kneeled in the mud. But how was that communicated? I don't know. Somehow it was *understood*. I know I sound fucking crazy right now. I could tell this story a thousand times, which I probably have by now — and I'll never not sound like a lunatic.

I wondered then — as I wonder now — if Jessica *was* saying something to him. Something too quiet for anyone else to hear. Her mouth wasn't moving, but also her mouth was made of water, so I don't think normal rules of biology applied here, exactly.

They remained like that so long, neither of them moving, I almost screamed when Jessica leaned over. Now they were face to face. She tilted her head a little, then pressed her liquid lips against his meaty lips. Never in a million years would I have expected her to kiss him, yet that's what she did.

From the opposite end of the yard, Trey shouted, "Dude, what the fuck are you doing?"

Gus also joined in. "I don't think this is an appropriate time for romance, son!" he yelled over the rain. For *romance*. [*Laughs.*]

The kiss lasted longer than any kiss I've never seen, in real life or a movie—and that's including porn, by the way. Yet there was nothing remotely sexual about it. Neither of them seemed to be enjoying themselves. At a certain point, Rick attempted to break free of the embrace, but it was like their mouths were glued together—intertwined, you know? It was then, as he struggled and failed to escape, that it became clear what was happening. She wasn't *just* kissing him. She was emptying herself into him. Pumping his body full of water—or whatever, exactly, comprised her DNA.

He stopped fighting. His body went limp. He was dead. Drowned. Yet…their mouths did not separate. The liquid continued flowing into his corpse. Neither Gus nor Trey tried to save him. They were too shocked to move. As was I. We were witnessing something out of this world. Maybe we could have stopped it—but also, deep down, maybe we didn't want to stop it. To interrupt this scene would have meant denying ourselves the privilege of experiencing something wholly unique and bizarre. And isn't that, in a way, what we are all searching for?

Well, Rick's body started bloating. It was full of water. The seal around his and Jessica's mouths was impenetrable. There was nowhere else for the water to go. So…yeah. I mean. You know what happened. We all know what happened. It was the only thing that *could* happen.

Rick exploded.

He fucking *exploded*.

And it was that explosion—that gruesome splattering of Rick's goopy insides—that weakened our trance. This was *real*. My sister, back from the dead, had blown up a man. A

The Last Haunt

kid, really, when you think about it. We were all kids—except for Gus.

Gus, who was now screaming and running away. Running *where,* though, I don't know. This was his property. This was his back yard. There was nowhere for him to go—but that didn't stop him from trying. I watched him flee across the yard, toward the closed fence gate. He almost made it, too. But the rain got him. My *sister* got him. His feet sunk into the earth, swallowed by the freshly-conjured mud, and his body hitched forward, falling face-first. Despite the storm, I could hear plain as day the sound of his ankles snapping, followed by the sound of his lungs unloading the loudest squeal I've ever heard come out of another human being.

Jessica started heading toward him. Her legs didn't appear to move, though. It was more like she glided across the yard. But then something stopped her. You remember the zombie gnome that'd been used to give me a concussion? It returned. This time, Trey *threw* the gnome. I don't know what he hoped to accomplish here. The figure hit my sister on the back. Instead of knocking her down, the gnome plunged into her body, like an object might enter a jello mold. There was this almost-comical beat where nobody moved. The gnome gestated within her midsection, slowly drooping down.

Then, Jessica was suddenly facing Trey. Yet—she didn't turn around. It was like her front features inverted and swapped with her back. [*Laughs.*] Does that make any sense? I'm sorry if I'm not articulating this well enough. You have to understand, this night was several years ago. Sometimes, when I think about it, it feels more like a dream I had than something I really experienced. But the same can be said for *all* of the outside world. How much of it truly exists, and how much of it have I fantasized?

I think Trey might've said something like, "Oh my god," or maybe, "Holy shit," before the gnome shot out of my sister's body like a slingshot and shattered against his head. He crumbled to the ground, splashing in the mud that was now so deep he practically disappeared in it. Later, when I found the strength and courage to stand, I would inspect his body and find tiny shards of ceramic poking out of his face and neck. Both of his eyes were...I guess *popped*—the sockets now occupied by pieces of the broken gnome. If he hadn't died from *that*, then most certainly he drowned from the rain and mud that had entered his open mouth as he lay there bleeding out.

Jessica returned her attention to Gus, who was still writhing and crawling toward the fence gate. He didn't seem to be making a lot of progress, though. For one thing, as I said, I'd heard his ankles break. Plus, the rain, the mud—it was not the easiest texture to maneuver through. She had him trapped. There was no rush. No hurry. I feel like, if she had so desired, she possessed the ability to make this night—this *moment*—stretch on forever.

Maybe the mud got too deep, or maybe he sensed Jessica hovering over him. I don't know why he rolled over on his back, but he did. He was screaming louder than the rain. Crying. *Begging*. Begging as so many of his haunt participants had begged to be let go. But, in true McKinley Manor fashion, there was no safe word here. There was no escape.

She straddled him, her watery legs merging with the mud beneath them. Gus didn't stop screaming until her mouth latched onto his and water drowned his lungs. His legs kicked out and then they stopped. He stopped fighting back. He stopped doing anything. The kiss continued. The water continued. There was nowhere for it go.

I'd already seen one person combust that night, but that didn't tame the shock when it happened again.

There, in the mud, beneath the vengeful spirit of my sister, Gus McKinley exploded.

One moment he was a person, a body full of guts and

The Last Haunt

organs and bones—and then, just like that, he was no longer any of those things.

He was nothing.

How, exactly, the police think I managed to do such a thing to a person still remains a mystery. They don't know *how*. They tried to figure it out, sure, but did they? It turns out it didn't really matter. The jury still convicted me, didn't they? And now here I am. Locked away for the rest of my life for something unexplainable.

After Gus was finished, Jessica turned her watery gaze upon me. There was never any fear that she'd do the same as she had to Gus and Rick. I knew she didn't mean me any harm. The reassuring comfort I'd felt when the rain first started coming down only strengthened as she neared. The blood from Gus and Rick had smeared into her liquid structure, further dirtying her translucence. When she was close enough, she reached out her hand. I stuck my own out and grabbed it, fully expecting my fingers to splash through hers. To my amazement, her hand was solid enough to grasp. She was *tangible*. She was *strong*. She pulled me to my feet. We were inches apart now. I should have said something, I *wanted* to say something, but I couldn't conceive of any words. Language had failed me. I could only hold her wet hand and stare into her aquatic eyes as the rain poured down upon us and the rest of the Manor.

I swear, for half a second, she managed to smile.

And then, with the abruption of a finger snap, it was over.

The rain stopped.

Jessica—my sister—whatever magic had been in place holding her together finally expired, and she spilled to the grass with the last final drops of rain from the clouds above. The only remnant of her arrival that night was the wetness trickling down my now-empty hand. Other than that, I was alone.

BETTY ROCKSTEADY

It was exactly like the year before, with that Jessica bitch. After Gus ended the haunt, I waited all night for him to call. I tried to reach him a few times myself, but it went straight to voicemail. I figured maybe his phone really *had* died, and he'd fallen asleep while waiting for it to charge. No big deal, right? These things happen. I tried not to let myself get too worked up about it, but it was hard. When it came to Gus, I worried easily. He was the love of my goddamn life, after all.

The next morning, I woke up to the news all over Facebook. I read everything there was to read. I tried to talk to people, but nobody wanted to hear from me. I didn't know what to do. I didn't know what had happened. Everything was so confusing. It was hard to believe. I'd just talked to him the previous day, and now he was gone? *Everything* was gone. Gus, the Manor, fucking everything.

JOHN BALTISBERGER

There ain't a doubt in my mind that the little pipsqueak did it. Anybody who theorizes otherwise is a delusional clown. Supernatural spirits from the dead made out of water? No, sir, I don't think so. I mean, take a look at his confession. He claims it rained that night. Rained so hard the mud broke Gus's ankles. Well, as we all know, thanks to the testimony of a local meteorologist—and, also, the eye-witness accounts of several Pork Basket residents—there was no evidence of it having rained. We had a dry Halloween that year. Everybody got to trick-r-treat until their hearts were content.

But listen. I don't need to prove he's lying. He needs to prove he's telling the truth, and in all these years he's never

The Last Haunt

been able to come up with one shred of evidence proving his innocence. You know why? He ain't innocent. He went to Gus's that night with one thing on his mind: revenge. And guess what? Mission accomplished. He did it. Now he's going to spend the rest of his life with that decision weighing down on him.

All I gotta say is, I hope it was worth it. I hope he feels satisfied with himself. I sure would hate to do something so extreme, so senselessly gruesome, only to regret my actions after the fact with no way to undo it. I can't imagine a worse hell.

DEBORAH KEATON

When I heard about what happened to Gus, I didn't believe it. I thought someone was pranking me—maybe Gus himself. I wouldn't have put it past him. To give me one last scare. But I asked around, and I confirmed it was the truth. How did I feel? I felt relieved. Does that make me a terrible person? I'm sure. But it's the truth. It wasn't until then that I genuinely felt like we could move on and begin a new life. There was no longer that...*anchor* holding us back. We were free.

I'm not naive. One day, I know Charlie's going to find out about all of this. But for right now, I'm choosing to keep him in the dark. It's why I insisted on using an alias for this interview. If I can hide the awful truth about his father for just another day, another month, another year, then I'll be satisfied.

I have to admit, though—every Halloween, when Charlie starts brainstorming how we're going to decorate the house, there's a certain dread that hits. I see that look in his eyes—that familiar excitement. I know what it means, and I hate it. I fucking *hate* it.

BETTY ROCKSTEADY

A week later, I deleted the Facebook group. A clean break. It was the only thing that made sense. I wasn't trying to cover anything up, as some people seem to believe. I just didn't want that reminder in my face every day. I wanted to be done with it, as impossible as that is. There's no *being done* with any of this. If there was, you wouldn't be here asking me all these questions. You wouldn't be writing your stupid book. Something like this, it never goes away. It haunts you forever.

CHRISTINE ADDAMS

I've heard the story—about the storm. I wish I could back him up there, but the truth is there wasn't a lick of rain on our street that night. My opinion on his innocence is not important, anyhow. Who cares if he's guilty? Maybe ask me if I think he was justified. Because hell fucking yes I do. Gus killed his *sister*. I know that other kid took the fall for it, but c'mon. You want to convince me Charles Manson was innocent, too?

TREVOR HENDERSON

I could tell you about those initial police interrogations. The trial. The tabloids. All that bullshit. But what's the point? I'm tired. I've said what I have to say. I've told the truth. Beyond that, everything else is out of my control.

That night, Jessica returned from the dead to do two things: save me, and exact revenge on those who had previously wronged her. Was it a perfect plan? No, not even close. In doing so, she ended up sentencing me to life imprisonment. But, you know, I don't know if someone in her condition could realistically *form* a real, coherent plan. Could she think like that? Could she...uh, *brainstorm*? I don't know. These things are too complicated and beyond our scope of reality to understand.

But I do know this.

Jessica did what she felt like she had to do—and, considering how she left this earth, I find it hard to be upset with her. The whole reason I volunteered to do the haunt that Halloween night was to get revenge, after all—to make things right for her. And, as morbid as it might sound, it's hard not to feel like we somehow accomplished that goal. The debt feels...*settled*.

So, believe what you want. You and anyone else reading this. Nothing is going to change what really happened. Nothing is going to take away from my sister's catharsis. I might be the one in prison, but in the grand scheme of things, none of this was ever about me. This was never my story.

It was Jessica's.

ZACH CHAPMAN

You know that night? Halloween night, man. Probably the exact same time of the massacre. I'd be willing to bet *money* on it. The same night, the same time—you want to know what was going on at the prison? What was going on in my fucking cell?

By then, it was already lights out. They don't let you roam around too late in the joint. The guards get jumpy. They get sick of looking at you all day. They make you go lie down. Which is what I was doing. I was lying down. I was in my bunk. Trying to sleep and failing, because I *knew*, man, I knew what the day was, I knew it was the anniversary of the worst thing I'd ever done in my life, and I was having a real rough time trying to process it. There was no fuckin' way I was gonna get to sleep that night.

And that was when I heard the noise—from across the cell. The toilet, man, it was doing something...*weird*. I hadn't used it in at least an hour, okay? The pipes had long settled by then. Also something to keep in mind: the prison toilets had that strong vacuum flushing. Those things were almost impossible to clog, unless you tried, like, stuffing your sheets down it or something.

So tell me why, suddenly, the toilet in my cell—and *only* the toilet in my cell—had decided to back up? When I looked down from my bunk, I saw water streaming from out of the rim. Just fucking *pouring* to the floor. I got up and tried shouting for the guards, but somehow the floor had already flooded, and I slipped, cracking my head good against the side of my bunk. When I looked up, I saw a motherfucking *fountain* of water spraying out of the toilet then, like a...like a *fire hydrant,* man, I shit you not. It was *strong*.

Luckily, a guard noticed the disturbance and got me out of there. Of course they blamed *me* for what had happened, accused me of doing something to destroy the toilet, and threw me in solitary for a couple days. That was fine by me, though. I had no desire to return to my cell. Because I knew I hadn't done anything to the toilet. That shit had happened by itself, you understand? Like...fucking *magic*, almost, you know?

Now imagine my fucking surprise—my fucking *horror*—when, a few days later, I discover that Gus had been killed on the very same night that I was dealing with my mysterious toilet issue? Not only that, but the boy they put the blame on is claiming the girl I killed—his fucking *sister*—came back as a fuckin' water ghost and flooded their bodies until they exploded?

There are things in this world that you can chalk up to coincidence. Not everything *means* something. I get that. I buy into that. But I also believe sometimes things *do* mean something, sometimes things *aren't* just a coincidence.

So do I think Trevor Henderson was telling the truth that night, about what happened at McKinley Manor?

I don't know, man — what the fuck do *you* think?

ABOUT THE AUTHOR

Max Booth III does not exist, and neither do you.

www.ghoulish.rip

Made in the USA
Coppell, TX
23 October 2023